BFFs

True Colours

For Sammy

STRIPES PUBLISHING
An imprint of Little Tiger Press
1 The Coda Centre, 189 Munster Road,
London SW6 6AW

A paperback original
First published in Great Britain in 2013

Text copyright © Belinda Rapley, 2013

ISBN: 978-1-84715-361-6

Printed and bound in the UK.

10 9 8 7 6 5 4 3 2 1

Holly Robbins

BFFs

True Colours

Stripes

Nisha gets a mysterious phone call...

"It's just down here!" Nisha called. "I'm sure it is!" She hurried round a corner and down a steep side street. We followed after her.

Jas wobbled and her arms windmilled for a second. She was wearing a pair of wedge-heeled boots that she'd got for Christmas. "If I'd known we were going hiking, I'd have worn different shoes," she giggled.

"I know the café's around here somewhere!" Nisha said uncertainly. There was no sign of it, though, so we followed her back up the hill, puffing, to the next street along.

"I hope the hot chocolates are worth it after all

this!" Lexie said, letting out a slightly hysterical laugh.

"It's not hot chocolates we're going to need at this rate," I added, starting to laugh with her. "It's Mountain Rescue!"

Nisha turned back to look at us and the next moment me and my three BFFs were giggling helplessly. We'd been shopping all morning, spending our Christmas money, and Nisha had persuaded us to go to her favourite hangout for a post-shopping drink. It was an art gallery, with its own little shop and café. Only Nisha normally went with her mum, and she'd forgotten which road it was on. *And* what it was called.

Nisha's face suddenly lit up. "Look, there it is! The Frame – now I remember!"

"On the *opposite* side of the street!" Lexie shook her head with a smile. "No wonder we couldn't find it – we were looking in the wrong direction!"

Still laughing, we linked arms and dashed across the road.

The gallery was warm and cosy. We had a quick look in the shop, then made for the café and ordered our drinks. There were posters stuck all over the brightly coloured walls and flyers were scattered on the table. I dumped my shopping bags on the floor and flopped gratefully onto the squishy sofa. It was so huge (compared to me, at least) that my feet didn't reach the floor. Jas sat down next to me and I went bouncing upwards, setting us off into a fresh wave of giggles.

As soon as the drinks arrived, I cupped my hands round the hot mug, warming up my frozen fingers, and tried to sip the thick chocolate through a mountain of marshmallows.

It was so nice to hang out with my BFFs and catch up. It was only the second time we'd seen each other over the holidays, so we had loads to talk about. We swapped stories about how we'd spent New Year's Eve and shared updates on whether we'd managed to stick to our New Year's resolutions so far … even though it was only the third of January! We'd met up at Lexie's house just before New Year, taking ages to think of them.

I glanced up at the posters and saw one that nearly made my eyes pop out of my head. "Ooh, is that your dad and his band, Nisha?"

Nisha had mentioned her dad's band to us a couple of times. Last year she'd been all set to go and see him play at our local venue, The Cornfield, but the

basement had flooded and the gig was cancelled. The manager found a last-minute change of venue, but it was miles away so Nisha had missed out. The band's name had stuck in my mind, and there it was on the poster – The Storm Chasers.

Nisha flushed slightly. She wasn't one to show off, but she looked really proud. "Yup, that's him!"

We all craned our necks to study the poster more closely. Nisha's dad was posing by a microphone. He had wild, backcombed hair and was wearing skinny jeans and a faded black T-shirt.

"Look! It says on the poster that he's playing at The Cornfield next month!" Jas exclaimed. "Do you think you'll get to see him this time?"

"Yep, it's all organized. Dad sent me tickets at Christmas!" Nisha beamed. "He had hoped he'd have time off at the end of this tour, but his manager's booked gigs across Europe straight afterwards. This will be the last chance I get to see him for ages. I'm so excited, I can't wait!"

We carried on slurping our drinks, rating them against the ones in the Ace Diner, mine and Jas's fave café. Then Lexie mentioned the new term at Priory Road. We were due back at school in three days.

True Colours

We all groaned.

"I wish the Christmas holidays lasted a bit longer, so we could all hibernate," Jas said, shivering as she looked out of the window at the grey sky. "I'd much rather be curled up under a duvet than running round on a hockey pitch!"

"I know. I'm *so* excited about running cross-country in all this freezing cold and mud," Lexie grimaced. "Not!"

As we chatted about school, I couldn't believe how chilled I felt about heading back to Priory Road. I'd been as wobbly as a jelly before starting Year Seven in September. I guess that's what being part of an awesome foursome of friends has done for my confidence!

Suddenly a mobile phone chirruped into life. Nisha fished about in her bag. "Weird, it's Mum... Hello? Yup, I'm still in town but I've finished shopping," she said. I could hear her mum's voice, but I couldn't make out what she was saying. "What, now? Oh, OK then, see you in a bit. Bye!"

Nisha put the phone down, frowning slightly.

"Is everything all right?" I asked, as she began to gather her bags together.

"I think so, but Mum's asked me to come home as soon as possible."

"Did she say why?" Lexie asked. "Did she sound cross or anything?"

"No, she sounded fine. She wouldn't say what it was about, though. She said she'd explain everything when I got home, but not to worry – it was something nice!"

"Oooh, cryptic!" Jas said.

I checked my watch and looked at Jas. "We'd better head off as well."

"Me, too, then, I guess!" Lexie added.

We grabbed our stuff and left The Frame, running to keep up with Nisha, who was power-walking to the bus stop.

"I wonder what the surprise is…" I said.

"Maybe your mum has bought you a puppy!" Lexie gasped. "We could both walk our dogs together!"

"I wish," Nisha grinned. "Dave's allergic, though, so it can't be that."

We ran the last stretch to the bus stop as we saw Lexie and Nisha's bus coming round the corner. Lexie got there first and leaped on. Nisha waited by the doors for a second, searching for her pass.

True Colours

"Don't forget to tell us what's going on as soon as you find out!" I said.

Nisha smiled. "Don't worry, I will!"

She jumped onboard and the doors closed with a hiss as the bus pulled away.

That evening after dinner I turned on the computer to see if I had any emails. Crumble, my huge tabby cat, lay spread out on my lap, like a furry hot-water bottle, purring with a deep, soft rattle. I logged on and saw Nisha was online, too. I sent her an instant message.

So...??????

I've been given a mission! Need help – r u free tomorrow?!

Yes! Y – what is it??!

Too long to explain now – c u here at 10? Will text Lexie n Jas xxx

Cu then! x

Mum and Dad were watching television, curled up on the sofa.

"Can I go to Nisha's tomorrow morning?" I asked.

"Have you got all your holiday homework finished?" Dad asked.

I nodded.

"OK then," Mum said. "As long as your room's tidy before you go. Are you doing anything special?"

"I don't know yet!" I smiled. "It's all a bit of a mystery!"

Nisha's on a mission... BFFs to the rescue!

"Your step-sister's coming to stay?" I said. We were sitting on Nisha's bed the next day, surrounded by a pile of soft toys. Nisha had just spilled the beans about why she'd had to rush home the day before. "I didn't even know you *had* a step-sister."

Nisha looked sheepish. "To be honest it doesn't often feel like I *have* got one," she admitted. "Poppy is Dave's daughter from before he married Mum. We're the same age, but I've only met her a couple of times. Once was at Mum and Dave's wedding, the other was when Callum was born, which was two years ago. Poppy lives in London now and normally Dave goes

down to visit her, she never comes up here."

"So, what's she like?" I asked.

"Well, from what I remember she was really nice," Nisha said.

"And she lives in London?" Lexie asked, sounding impressed.

"That's where my dad lives," Jas said proudly. "I wonder if they're from the same area? I've been there a few times – we might even know the same places!"

"Jas, London's massive, it's pretty unlikely," Lexie joked.

Jas shrugged, as she sat with her long gangly legs tucked under her. "I can still ask her," she said, fiddling with a fluffy owl that was on Nisha's bed.

Jas had been my BFF since the first day of nursery – literally! We could read each other like a book and I could see that Jas was a bit upset by what Lexie had said. Jas hardly ever saw her dad, so any link was precious to her, however small.

"So how come Poppy's coming here, then?" I asked, changing the subject.

"Poppy's grandmother lives in Australia," Nisha explained. "She had a fall and she's in hospital. Poppy's mum is flying out there to see her."

True Colours

"Do you know how long Poppy's staying?" Lexie asked.

"About a week, Dave reckons, although he's not really sure," Nisha said.

I looked around. Nisha's house was really cosy and full of character, but it wasn't very big. "Where's she going to sleep?"

"Well, we don't have a spare bedroom," Nisha explained, "so she'll be sharing with me. It's a bit small, but Mum and Dave thought that would be most fun for us both!"

"You're so lucky!" I beamed. "It'll be like a permanent sleepover!" I'm an only child and sometimes I wish I had a brother or sister. "Are you excited?"

Nisha nodded, but she looked more thoughtful than excited. "I guess it's a bit weird that someone I don't really know is going to be staying, but I hope it'll be fun. And that's where you guys come in. Mum and Dave have given me a mission. Poppy's likely to find this all really strange, too, so they've asked me to try and make her feel at home. I was hoping you might be able to help out with that bit – I'm feeling a bit clueless about where to start!"

"We need a plan!" Jas said, her momentary upset forgotten.

"When's she getting here?" I asked.

"Well, it's all been totally last minute. Dave went to pick her up this morning," Nisha said, glancing at the alarm clock on her bedside table, "so she should be here in a few hours!"

"OMG!" Jas gasped, making a mock-horror face. "We don't just need a plan – we need a *superfast* plan! Come on!"

We didn't have time to go all the way into town, so instead we raided the local shops for things to brighten up Nisha's room. Nisha didn't have a clue what Poppy liked, so we grabbed lots of little things to try and cover all bases. While we'd been out, Nisha's mum, Jamila, had put up a swish camp bed in Nisha's room.

"I think I'm going to give Poppy my bed," Nisha said, after we'd tried the camp bed in about a hundred positions. In the end we thought it looked best by the window. "I mean, the camp bed's pretty comfy and Poppy's probably only staying for a week."

Once she'd made that decision, we worked like

16

crazy to transform Nisha's room into a welcoming den, with one eye on the ticking clock.

After we'd finished we stood back to admire our efforts. Nisha had chosen her duvet cover and pillow set with hearts on. We'd arranged the soft toys along the end of the bed, and put her "Love" cushion by the pillow. A brand-new copy of the latest *Fab Girl!* magazine lay on the bed, along with a stuffed bag of pick 'n' mix sweets and some sparkly pink flower-shaped hair clips. We'd agonized over the choices for ages in the shop. The glitter-tastic banner we'd made swung from Nisha's bookshelf, with "Welcome Poppy!" emblazoned across it. Nisha had packed away her summer stuff in a suitcase and put it under her bed, so there was space in the wardrobe for Poppy to hang up her things.

"We are awesome!" Jas exclaimed.

"Just one more finishing touch," Nisha said. She bent down and rearranged the small rug to sit next to the bed. As she stood back up we heard a car in the drive.

"Nisha!" Jamila called up the stairs, sounding slightly nervous. "I think they're here!"

Nisha glanced once more at the room.

"Poppy will love it!" I reassured her.

"Fingers crossed," she said. "Here goes!"

We piled downstairs just as Dave walked through the door. Behind him stood a girl about the same height as Lexie and Nisha. She was pretty and effortlessly cool, with spiky, elfin-cut hair the same auburn as Dave's. Her denim shorts were so skimpy that the pockets were hanging down below the cut-off and she had on thick black tights, a black biker jacket, chunky boots and silver rings on her fingers. Her skin was pale and her huge eyes were made bigger by black eyeliner. The only thing that didn't seem to go with her outfit was a fine gold chain with a heart-shaped locket on the end of it, which hung outside her top. I smiled at her, and the others did the same. Poppy leaned towards Dave, half returning the smile.

"Everyone, this is Poppy," Dave announced, one hand on her shoulder. "Poppy, do you remember Nisha?"

"Hi!" Nisha said, stepping forward. Her step-sister looked at Nisha coolly.

"Poppy?" Dave prompted her.

Poppy gave him a look. "Hi," she said, without smiling. Nisha was a bit wrong-footed, but pressed on and introduced us anyway.

"We've been helping to get your room ready," Jas explained.

"Cool," Poppy replied flatly.

"You must be tired," Jamila said, breezing forward through the tension and giving her a kiss on the cheek. Poppy smiled faintly at her and nodded. "And hungry. Why don't you take your stuff upstairs, then we can eat."

"OK, thanks, Jamila," Poppy said politely. I had been hoping that our welcome efforts would put a smile on her face, but I was starting to panic about what she'd make of them. After all, we'd expected someone just like us, but Poppy couldn't have appeared more different!

"I don't know if you remember my room – it's been forever since your last visit…" Nisha said as we went upstairs. "Well, at least two years."

Poppy shrugged, lugging her bag unenthusiastically.

Nisha glanced at us before she pushed open her bedroom door. "Anyway, I'm really pleased you're here."

"It's not like I had any choice," Poppy said, as she stepped into the room. She glanced around, taking in the banner and our other little touches.

"You're having my bed," Nisha explained. "I'm going to sleep on the camp bed."

"We're sharing?" Poppy frowned. "Are you serious?"

Nisha nodded, biting her lip.

Poppy sighed and dumped her bag on the floor. Then she noticed the magazine and smiled. For a second I thought we'd cracked it…

Until Poppy spoke, that was. "*Fab Girl!*? I stopped reading that ages ago. Can't you get *Teen Talk* here?"

"Of course we can!" Lexie said defensively. By the look on Lexie's face, her first impressions of the new arrival weren't great.

"It's just, Mum says it's a bit old for me," Nisha said.

Poppy made a face. Her eyes moved to the end of the bed. "Um, can I move these?" she asked, picking up a soft, floppy puppy. "They're … kind of … a bit young."

Jas looked like she wanted to explode at Nisha's step-sister, but I shoved a fluffy kitten at her and she was momentarily distracted. We all helped Nisha to move the mountain of soft toys on to the floor by her camp bed. Poppy moved the packet of sweets like they

20

were radioactive and put them on her bedside table. She sat down on the bed with a sigh and crossed her arms. We all stood there and Nisha looked at us, unsure what to do next. This was not going the way we'd planned – at all.

The tension was broken when Dave appeared at the door. "Are you girls ready for some food?"

"I'm a bit shattered, actually, Dad," Poppy said, through a yawn. "Do you mind if I just stay up here for a bit?"

"Of course not, you've had a tiring day." Dave gave her a kiss on the top of her head. "Come down when you're ready."

"Um, we better get going," Lexie said, looking like she couldn't wait to get out of there. The rest of us rushed down the stairs after her.

We said goodbye to Mr and Mrs Harris and slipped out. I saw Nisha's face as she closed the front door behind us and I couldn't help feeling like we were abandoning her.

It's going to be a loooooooong week for Nisha...

"Maybe Poppy will be in a better mood today," I whispered to Jas, as we waited to order our drinks in the Ace Diner.

"She can't be in a worse one," Jas replied.

We'd agreed to meet up with Poppy and Nisha in town to hang out. It was our last day of freedom before going back to school. The teachers had an inset day so term started on Tuesday.

Poppy ambled in after Nisha, wearing a loose-fitting short black dress with a skull-and-crossbones print on it. She took no notice of Nisha's invitation to sit next to her and Lexie. Instead, she slid along the bench on mine and Jas's side of the booth, her leather jacket squeaking on the red vinyl of the seat.

She looked round, unimpressed. "I completely forgot what this town is like," she said. "It's tiny compared to London!"

"I know," Jas agreed knowledgably. "My dad lives there, too."

"Really, which part?" Poppy asked, suddenly brightening.

"Um, near Tooting?"

"Oh, right," Poppy said. "I live in Notting Hill, other side of town. Do you go to Oxford Circus much? Me and my best friend, Angel, go to Topshop all the time!"

"No, I haven't been there," Jas replied.

"What about the South Bank? They've got a cool skateboarding area there."

"Nope," Jas said, starting to squirm a bit. I could tell she wished she hadn't started the conversation.

"Have you been up the Olympic viewing tower yet? That's awesome, you can see for miles!"

"Actually, I've only been to London a couple of times," Jas confessed. "I don't see Dad very often, and when I do we pretty much stay in Tooting."

"You're *so* missing out," Poppy smiled, shaking her

head. "Meet up with me next time, I'll show you round properly! Sooo, what kinds of things *are* there to do around here?"

"Loads," Lexie piped up. "There's ice skating, the cinema, oh, and there's a skateboarding park near here, too."

"There's a swimming pool," Nisha added. "And a bowling alley. And we're always going to each other's houses for sleepovers and stuff. We have lots of fun, don't we?"

We nodded as Nisha looked round at me, Jas and Lexie. Poppy pulled a face. "Aren't there any clubs or anything?"

"What, do you mean like Guides?" Nisha asked.

Poppy giggled into her drink. "Not exactly. There's this under-sixteens club just down the road from me and Angel," she explained, looking at me, Lexie and Jas. "We go there loads at the weekend. We've just started at this street dance group, too. We're really into urban stuff."

As Poppy talked about her ultra-exciting life, Nisha kept trying to join in, but Poppy pretty much ignored her. I swirled my hot chocolate, my face blushing slightly. I was beginning to feel uncool, with my sparkly hairband and my neat Christmas-present jeans. I didn't

even really get what urban stuff was, not that I was
about to admit that!

"And we go to the Notting Hill Carnival, too," Poppy
added. "Like, every year. I stay at Angel's house lots as
well, when Mum's working. Angel's pretty wild. Her
mum lets us stay up so late, listening to all her music."

"Snap. We do that at sleepovers, too," Jas chipped
in. "We made up the best dance ever to 'Free' – that
was our fave song last term. We could show you?"

For a second I thought Jas was about to launch
into the moves, but Poppy's burst of laughter soon put
a stop to that.

"Not *that* kind of music," she said, bringing the
conversation back to her again. "I meant *cool* music,
you know, like dance anthems. That's what everyone in
my school is raving about."

Me and Jas exchanged a confused look – neither of
us had a clue what Poppy was on about, but Nisha
beamed.

"I love listening to new music!" she said, jumping at
the chance to join in. "Maybe you could play some
when we get back home?"

Poppy made a face. "It's kind of a 'me and Angel'
thing."

Nisha looked surprised and hurt. I gave her a small smile and Lexie quickly changed the subject.

"So, have you got lots of homework and stuff for this week?"

"None!" Poppy grinned. "Thankfully! School have said that, as these are 'exceptional circumstances', I don't have to worry about work this week. I just get to hang out with Dad. He's manically busy at work, finalizing a big, important pitch for a new customer at his advertising agency. But he's managed to wangle a week off just for me – it's going to be awesome! Anyway, where are the loos in this place?"

Lexie pointed them out and Poppy sauntered away. Nisha let a tiny sigh slip out.

"What was last night like?" Lexie whispered. "Did she ever stop talking about herself?"

Nisha squirmed a bit. "Um, she was fine, really," she said. "She was pretty tired, so we didn't talk. She just went straight to sleep."

Jas began to tell us about a dream she'd had the night before. She'd been given a book about the meaning of dreams for Christmas and she thought that her dream meant that she was destined to be on the stage. We were all coming up with different interpretations for the dream, joking around and teasing Jas about her obsession with being famous. "Nisha, what do you think?" Jas asked, realizing that Nisha wasn't joining in the conversation.

"What? Oh, sorry, I was just thinking about something else…" She smiled sheepishly at us and looked towards the toilets anxiously. It seemed like she was worrying about Poppy, and I didn't blame her. Poppy was being fine with me, Lexie and Jas, but it was a different matter with Nisha. Whenever Nisha had tried to join in, Poppy pretty much blanked her.

"Are you OK, Nisha?" I asked.

"Yes, I'm fine. I'm just not sure Poppy likes me, that's all. It's probably nothing. I think I'm worrying too much!" Nisha replied.

"Maybe Poppy's just feeling a bit unsure about everything," I suggested.

"That's what Mum said last night," Nisha said, forcing a smile. "She said it must be unsettling for Poppy to be uprooted like this."

"But I bet she'll be fine by tomorrow," I said, trying to sound encouraging.

Nisha nodded, but she didn't seem completely convinced.

Spring term at Priory Road started in a manic rush. I struggled out of bed and put on my uniform.

"Mum! Dad!" I rushed down the stairs and into the kitchen.

"Where's the fire?!" Dad joked, finishing off his toast.

"Look! Do you think I've grown a bit?"

One of my biggest fears when I'd started at Priory Road was how silly I'd look in my oversized uniform. Luckily, I wasn't the only Year Seven whose parents had decided to buy uniform that could be "grown into". Even so, I still couldn't wait for it to shrink (or for me to get bigger) and right now I was convinced that my skirt was looking less like a tent.

"Maybe." Mum smiled, and Dad ruffled my hair as he grabbed his packed lunch from the sideboard and headed for the door.

Time felt like it was on fast-forward as I raced around to get everything ready for school. I wolfed down some breakfast and then began chucking books into my bag and looking for my pencil case. Once I'd found everything I kissed Mum goodbye and raced over to Jas's. She lived just round the corner and we always walked to the bus stop together.

When we got to our classroom it was buzzing with chatter. Miss Dubois, our form teacher, called for order and then asked us how our holidays were – in French! We had to answer in French, too – groan... Ed cracked everyone up (except for frosty-face Kirsty, who never laughs for fear of inducing wrinkles) by saying everything in English with a really strong French accent. Ajay and Dev told everyone about their band practices. They'd been inspired by the great reaction they'd got at the talent show last term and had started rehearsing loads of new songs! Kirsty went into detail about a makeover party, all in English, despite Miss Dubois's protests.

After a painful morning of lessons, where one homework task was piled on to another, we finally reached lunchtime. Lexie reluctantly disappeared off for netball practice. Me, Jas and Nisha moved towards the dining hall with the rest of the noisy crowd and managed to get a table in the corner near our friends, Zophia, Molly, Tabitha and Trin.

Jas thumbed through the homework list. "Ugh, Poppy's so lucky missing all this work!"

"What's she up to today?" I asked Nisha.

"I think Mum and Dave have taken her and Callum to the zoo," Nisha said, then quickly changed the subject.

I didn't mention Poppy again after that, as Nisha seemed keen to talk about anything other than what was going on at home. I hoped that everything would settle down, because Nisha definitely didn't seem her usual cheery self.

The rest of the day flew by. Some lessons carried on where they'd left off before Christmas, like the break had never happened. In others we were set completely new projects. In art Miss Malik gave us a fashion task. We had to design our very own high-street outfit, including shoes and accessories.

Kirsty almost fell off her stool with excitement. "OMG, this is fate!" She clapped her hands.

"Fate?" Miss Malik enquired.

Kirsty didn't need any prompting. "Yes!" She looked round the class to check who was listening. "Because in a few weeks' time I'm modelling with my best friend Eliza in an actual catwalk fashion show! This project is so perfect for me. I might even become a designer one day – if I don't end up modelling, that is!"

Miss Malik smiled. "I hope everyone else is as enthusiastic about the project as Kirsty."

It was fair to say that most of the boys were not.

"This is for girls, miss!" Zac complained. He looked disgruntled as our teacher showed us big pasteboards with proper designs to inspire us.

"Do you know that many top designers are male, Zac? I'm sure you've heard of Ralph Lauren and Giorgio Armani," Miss Malik pointed out. "Now, start to think about your designs, please."

Nisha looked worried. Art was her favourite – and her best – subject, but she whispered that this sort of project wasn't her kind of thing. "I don't know anything about fashion!" she said.

"That's OK," I said. "Neither do I. At least you can draw well. When I try and draw people they end up looking like yetis!"

Nisha giggled. We went over to look at the samples Miss Malik had put out, and by the time the bell rang, Nisha had lots of ideas for her project and had forgotten that she had ever been worrying about it. We packed up our stuff, then headed for the main hall.

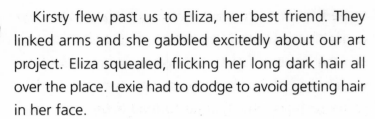

Kirsty flew past us to Eliza, her best friend. They linked arms and she gabbled excitedly about our art project. Eliza squealed, flicking her long dark hair all over the place. Lexie had to dodge to avoid getting hair in her face.

"Mum asked if I could skip drama club tonight to spend time at home with Poppy," Nisha confessed, as we trooped along the corridors with Zophia, Trin and Molly. "But I didn't want to – I really enjoy drama. Is … is that a bit mean?"

"No!" me and Jas both exclaimed in unison, then grinned.

"Dad asked me if I wanted to go back to swimming at the club twice a week," I added, as we went into the main hall, "instead of coming to drama club, now the play's over. I told him the same thing!"

There were lots of familiar faces from the school Christmas production, *Oliver!,* as well as some new people. I groaned – one of them was Ed! Although, as Lexie pointed out, he had been pretty hilarious in the talent show. He goofed about during the warm-up exercises, making everyone laugh. Mrs Crawfield told him he was a born comedian, although I'm not sure it was meant as a compliment! Once she'd managed to settle everyone down, she told us about the new project for this term. We were going to be interpreting key scenes from Shakespeare's plays in groups of four. Once everyone had got into groups, we were given a scene to work on. We had to read it through, then come up with our own version of it. We were given the scene with the three witches from *Macbeth*. It took ages to work out what it meant, but once we'd done that it was actually quite fun. Jas started leaping around and pretending to be a toad that had hopped out of a witch's cauldron!

Once the club had finished, we started to make our way out. But Nisha was hanging back.

"Come on, Nish," Lexie said impatiently, "my dinner'll be getting cold!"

"I'm going as fast as I can," Nisha mumbled, grabbing her bag. We stepped out into the dark, cold evening, and headed for the bus stop. I noticed Dave's car and I was sure that Nisha had seen it, too, but she kept walking towards the bus stop.

"Nish, look, Dave's over there," I pointed out.

"Oh, really?" she said, pretending that she hadn't realized. Then I glimpsed Poppy in the front passenger seat. She was smiling and chatting away, but as soon

as she saw Nisha her face fell and she looked the other way.

"See you tomorrow," Nisha said a bit glumly, before walking to the car.

A seriously unexpected situation develops...

Towards the end of the first week, Nisha finally started to let slip snippets of what life was like sharing a room with Poppy. There were other issues, apart from the fact that Poppy was only interested in talking about herself.

"She was in a serious grump last night," Nisha confessed at lunchtime on Thursday. "Her mum called and said that her nan wasn't doing so well, and that she might have to stay a bit longer. Poppy basically demanded that she came home anyway! Then she just sat upstairs listening to music with her headphones on for the rest of the evening."

Nisha pushed her lunch around her plate, lost in thought. "And it's stressful sharing a room with her – she's so messy! Her make-up's everywhere and she just chucks her clothes all over the floor. She's totally taken over my bedroom!"

"Are you OK, Nisha?" Trin asked. She, Zophia, Molly and Tabitha were sharing our table in the packed, noisy canteen.

"She's having step-sister issues," Lexie said. "They'll be sorted soon though. As soon as Poppy's gone!"

Nisha looked a bit embarrassed as Zophia and the others exchanged glances.

"It looks like you need a hot chocolate topped with cream and marshmallows to de-Poppy you," Jas said to Nisha after she'd sighed for about the hundredth time that day. "Who votes we go to The Frame after school?"

We called our parents from the bus to let them know where we were. It was pretty obvious from Nisha's side of the conversation that her mum was not impressed.

"What did your mum say?" I asked.

"This is the stop!" Jas interrupted. She jumped up and pressed the bell. We rushed down the stairs as the bus lurched to a halt.

True Colours

"Mum said I should have invited Poppy," Nisha said, making a face. "Now I feel bad – should I phone her back and ask her?"

"No!" Lexie said bluntly. "If you're anything to go by, she's a serious mood dampener!"

Nisha giggled guiltily. "I just don't think I can take any more talk about how amazing her life is!"

We jumped off the bus and walked quickly to the café. We ordered our drinks and carried them over to the comfy sofas.

"Is Poppy really that bad?" I asked.

"She is pretty self-centred, but I can cope with that bit, really. It's the other stuff that's just a bit weird."

"Like what?" Jas frowned, fishing out a marshmallow with her fingers.

"Well, when I get home after school she's always laughing and joking with Dave," Nisha explained, "or cooking with Mum or playing with Callum. But if I try to be nice to her or join in she makes an excuse and does something else. And when we're on our own in the bedroom she just totally blanks me. I've tried hard to get along with her, but it's really uncomfortable. She's making me feel like *I'm* the outsider in the house, not her."

"Have you talked to your mum about it?" I asked. "That's what I'd do."

Nisha shook her head and sank deeper into the sofa. "Mum's been pretty stressed this week trying to keep everyone happy. I didn't want to make it any harder for her, so I've kept quiet about it."

"At least it *is* only for a week," Lexie said. "You've only got a couple more days to go!"

"Fingers crossed," Nisha grimaced. "Speaking of which, Mum was wondering if you all fancied coming for a sleepover on Saturday, as it will probably be Poppy's last night?" She looked round at us all a bit desperately.

We all nodded.

"Thanks, guys," Nisha smiled. "I don't think I could have got through this week without my BFFs!"

We started thinking up activities for the sleepover.

"We could have a makeover party," I suggested. I'd learned how to put on make-up as part of the backstage crew in the school production last term, and I'd got my own little make-up case for Christmas.

"I could bring my karaoke machine, too," Jas added.

"That way there'll be plenty to distract Poppy if she's

38

in a funny mood!" Lexie agreed. "And if she gets too annoying, we could start a pillow fight to keep her quiet!"

Nisha giggled. "Could you imagine Poppy having a pillow fight? I reckon she'd think that was way too babyish!"

Nisha was pretty much waiting on the doorstep when I arrived for the sleepover with Jas and Lexie. "I'm so pleased you're here!" she said, dragging us into the warm house.

We waved bye to Dad and followed Nisha into her small hallway. Callum, her little brother, ran up to see who'd arrived and Jas tickled him, making him squirm and drop to the floor. We dumped all our overnight gear down just as Poppy came out of the kitchen, carrying a tray of chocolate muffins. They were freshly made, if the smell was anything to go by.

"Hi," she said to us with a smile. We followed her into the living room and she put the tray of muffins down. She looked really relaxed and at home. "Dig in!"

"Fab! Thanks, Poppy!" Lexie grinned.

"Callum helped me make these," Poppy said, winking at her half-brother. "Didn't you?"

Callum jumped up off the floor at once and grabbed a muffin. He shoved as much as he could fit into his mouth. "Mmmmmm!" he said, grinning and showing us his chocolatey teeth to prove how tasty they were. "Me and Poppy make muffins!"

"Urgh! Callum!" Nisha laughed, going to wipe his face.

He wriggled away from her and Poppy quickly picked him up. "It doesn't matter about a few crumbs, does it?" she said, smiling at him.

Nisha frowned, looking a bit hurt.

At that moment, Jamila appeared at the door. "Come on, Callum, let's leave the girls to their sleepover. And could you start by taking your stuff upstairs, please, girls!"

Poppy carried Callum into the kitchen. The rest of us headed to Nisha's bedroom. After what Nisha had been telling us, I expected it to be a state, but Poppy's side of the room was immaculate. Her plain black suitcase was sitting in the corner of the room, with just a few clean clothes neatly folded on top. There wasn't a trace of make-up or mess anywhere.

True Colours

"She was awake really early this morning," Nisha whispered. "She had almost finished packing before I woke up. Dave told her to wait until they heard the latest on her nan, but she wouldn't – she's totally convinced she's leaving tomorrow!"

"Maybe that's why she's in such a good mood," Jas suggested. "Because she can't wait to go home?"

"I guess your mum's right," I said, "it's probably been a difficult week for her."

Nisha nodded. "I know."

At that moment Poppy walked in, and we started comparing what make-up each of us had, nibbling at the chocolate muffins whilst we chatted.

Poppy put her iPod on and played us the Ibiza tunes her and Angel listened to when they got ready for the under-16s club. She refused to listen to Nisha's "naff" CDs, which we all loved!

"These muffins are awesome, I'm so stuffed!" Jas said, licking the crumbs off her lips. "Thanks, Poppy."

Poppy had loads more make-up than the rest of us put together, and she showed us how she put it on. "A makeover party is such a cool idea for a sleepover," she said. "I love it!"

Lexie was the first guinea pig and she wasn't

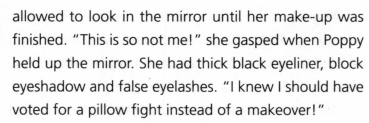

allowed to look in the mirror until her make-up was finished. "This is so not me!" she gasped when Poppy held up the mirror. She had thick black eyeliner, block eyeshadow and false eyelashes. "I knew I should have voted for a pillow fight instead of a makeover!"

"As if!" Poppy giggled. "But look, that make-up doesn't exactly go with a hoody and a scruffy pony tail. Time to tackle your hair!"

Soon we all had new looks. Poppy had loads of ideas for how we could get creative with our hair. She even helped me with Nisha's makeover, too. Poppy was being a lot nicer than I'd expected after everything Nisha had said. She'd tried really hard with the muffins and with the makeovers. When she stopped going on about London, she was actually lots of fun to hang out with!

We'd just carried Jas's karaoke machine downstairs to the living room, ready to rock our new looks, when the phone rang. A few minutes later Dave popped his head round the door, looking serious.

"Poppy, your mum's on the phone. She'd like to have a word."

"On the phone? Is she at the airport? What time's her flight?" Poppy jumped up and followed Dave out of the room.

"Listen, Poppy," we heard Dave say, "we talked about Mum maybe having to stay away for a bit longer, didn't we?"

We stood at the door, listening to the hushed whispers coming from the kitchen. Then we heard Poppy say hi to her mum. Next thing, she suddenly raised her voice.

"No way!" she cried. "If Nan's still unwell, why can't I fly out and join you?" There was a pause. "Can't I go and stay with Angel, then? I don't want to stay *here*! Are you *joking*? This is so unfair!"

The receiver crashed down and heavy footsteps ran up the stairs.

"Poppy!" Dave called out.

"Just leave me alone!" Poppy shouted back. The next second the bedroom door slammed shut and Poppy's music blasted into life.

We all looked round at each other.

Jamila came into the room. "Sorry to interrupt, girls," she said, forcing a smile. "Could we have a quick word, Nisha?"

"'Course," Nisha said, following her mum out.

"Sounds like Poppy might not be leaving tomorrow

after all," Jas whispered, turning off the karaoke machine.

We sat down, wondering what was going to happen next. Nisha came back in and sat down on the sofa next to Lexie.

"So, is Poppy staying, then?" I asked.

Nisha nodded. "Her gran's taken a turn for the worse, so that means Poppy's going to be here indefinitely. She can't stay off school any longer, so Poppy starts at Priory Road on Monday. Dave and Poppy's mum had already checked with school, in case something like this happened."

Things get even trickier for Nisha, and Kirsty gets some competition!

Dave dropped Nisha and Poppy off at Priory Road on Monday morning before heading to work. Nisha had texted us the night before and asked us to meet them at the gates so we could all walk in together. Me and Jas arrived first – we had caught an earlier bus just to make sure we were there on time. Lexie's bus must have been running late because she still hadn't arrived when Dave's car pulled up. Nisha waved as she saw us and came over. Poppy was still in the car, head down while Dave talked to her.

"Everything OK?" I asked, wondering how her Sunday had been after the bombshell was dropped at

the sleepover. Not that it *was* a sleepover in the end. We had all gone home, to give Nisha and her family some time on their own.

"Yup," Nisha said. "Last week was disastrous, but it's a new week and I'm going to make a fresh start with Poppy. She's going to be here for a while, so I'm determined to get along with her and make it as nice as possible."

At that moment, Poppy climbed out of the car, looking up at the school sullenly. It was obvious that she'd spent most of the night awake or crying because her eyes were puffy. Even without her trademark make-up, and with puffy eyes, she was still strikingly pretty. She looked uber-cool, too, because she wasn't wearing our dorky uniform. She had on thick black tights, a short, faded denim skirt, her boots and Nisha's spare Priory Road jumper over a white T-shirt. I felt like a grade-A geek next to her.

"Oh, we're not allowed to wear jewellery," I pointed out, noticing Poppy's delicate heart-shaped locket hanging over her jumper. "You might want to leave that with Dave…"

Poppy quickly tucked it away. "There are no stupid rules like that at my school," she said, frowning defiantly, "so that's tough. Anyway, I never take this off."

Me and Jas exchanged a look. Poppy clearly didn't share Nisha's positive outlook about her extended stay.

"Now, remember, Nisha," Dave said, winding down the window and leaning over to them. "Me and Mum want you to take care of Poppy, OK?"

"I don't need babysitting," Poppy snapped.

"I know that, sweetheart," Dave said, "but until you know your way round, I want you and Nisha to stick together. Understood?"

Poppy rolled her eyes and stomped off, joining the slowly moving crowd heading in through the double doors.

"I'll look out for her," Nisha reassured Dave. "Promise."

"So will we, Mr Harris," Jas added, just as Lexie ran up to us, breathless.

"Where's Poppy?" she asked.

"Already heading in," I said.

"Wow, she's keen."

"Come on," I said, grabbing Jas's arm as I saw Poppy disappearing in through the doors. "We don't want to lose her before the first lesson's even started!"

"*Attention fils et filles!*" Miss Dubois clapped her hands. Poppy was standing next to her by the front desk. "We have a new pupil joining us in Kingfisher from today."

Miss Dubois hadn't really needed to make that announcement. There wasn't a single person who hadn't noticed Poppy. Some of the boys were showing off more than normal and Zac tipped his chair back so far it slipped from under him and he landed with a thud on the floor. I saw Kirsty clock the boys' behaviour and roll her eyes.

"Everyone, this is Poppy Harris, Nisha's step-sister," Miss Dubois said. "She's here from London for a few weeks and I want everyone to make her feel very welcome."

Most of our classmates exchanged impressed glances and peered round to get a better look at Poppy, as she made her way to a seat. With her London vibe and her non-uniform coolness, it was like some kind of chic alien had landed! Trin and Molly gave her a welcoming smile. Ed had gone back to his history textbook. He was hurriedly trying to finish the homework Mr Wood set.

True Colours

"Sit here if you like?" Kirsty said, offering her the chair that Zophia normally sat in.

"Great, thanks, Kirsty!" Zophia huffed, overhearing her as she walked in a couple of minutes late.

"She's sitting next to me, anyway," Nisha said. Poppy was still in a mega-grump. She sat down, seemingly unaware of the stir she was causing. Lexie pulled up a spare chair and sat on the end of the desk next to Nisha.

"Now, Kingfisher," Miss Dubois said when she'd finished calling the register. "There will be a Valentine's disco on the last day of this half term. I'm passing round the forms now. If you plan to come, I will need this form to be signed by your parents and returned to me by the end of next week."

A murmur rippled round the classroom, as everyone began to talk about the disco.

"Is it for *all* years, miss?" Kirsty asked. Miss Dubois nodded and Kirsty actually looked excited.

"Thinking about all the Year Nines she can dance with, I bet!" Jas giggled to me.

"Oooh, I so don't want to see that!" I giggled. The thought of dancing with *anyone* made me feel nervous, let alone a Year Nine!

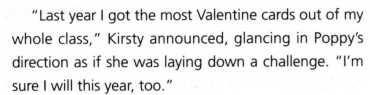

"Last year I got the most Valentine cards out of my whole class," Kirsty announced, glancing in Poppy's direction as if she was laying down a challenge. "I'm sure I will this year, too."

"What about me?" Ed piped up. "I might get more than you, you never know!" This set everyone off laughing. He knew as well as the rest of us that he'd be lucky to get any!

Jas's bony elbow poked me in the ribs.

"Ow! What?!"

"Don't look now, but Ed's staring right at you!"

Of course the first thing I did was look up. And Jas was right! Ed looked away quickly, but not before he'd seen me turn beetroot red – but only because Jas had embarrassed me. I so hoped he hadn't got the wrong idea and thought I'd blushed because I liked him… I mean, he was funny and goofy, but there was no way I liked him like THAT!

As the bell went for our first lesson, double PE, Miss Dubois called to Nisha, me, Jas, Lexie and Poppy to wait behind.

"Poppy, I hope you enjoy your time at Priory Road," Miss Dubois said. "If you have any problems, you can talk to me, *oui*?"

True Colours

"*Oui, madame,*" Poppy nodded. Miss Dubois beamed.

"*Bon,*" she replied. "Now, Nisha and Lexie, I know that you sit with each other for most lessons, but I'd like it if Nisha could sit with Poppy for the moment and be her buddy. Lexie, I hope that's OK?"

Poppy caught the look that passed between Lexie and Nisha and registered their disappointment before looking at the floor.

"I'll let the other teachers know this is what's happening, too. And girls, I want you all to show Poppy round – make sure she gets to lessons on time and knows where to get lunch and drinks," Miss Dubois continued. "We're sorting out a locker for you, Poppy, so you can leave your books in there from tomorrow. *D'accord.* Any questions?" We all shook our heads. "*Bon.* To PE, *allez!*"

Poppy didn't have a swimming costume, so she had to sit and watch from the sidelines. I noticed that the boys put extra effort into their races, showing off in front of their new audience. Lexie gave up her normal seat next to Nisha in history and geography, so that Poppy could sit with her. Poppy edged the chair as far away as she possibly could, like Nisha had the lurgy.

At breaktime we trailed after Nisha as she showed Poppy the lockers, the loos and the dining hall. She took her assignment very seriously, and didn't notice how wound up Poppy was getting with the constant nannying.

By lunchtime Poppy had had enough. "I'm going to the loo," she announced.

"Oh, I'll come with you," Nisha smiled.

"I *don't* need to be escorted to the toilet!" Poppy said, finally breaking.

"Oh, OK, well, we'll save you a chair in the dining hall," Nisha said quietly. Poppy stalked off. Nisha stood looking anxiously down the corridor for a second.

"Maybe Poppy just needs some space, Nish," Lexie suggested. "You don't literally need to hold her hand all day."

"I was just trying to be helpful," Nisha said.

"You *are* being helpful," I said, not wanting Nisha to feel bad. "I'm sure Poppy appreciates it."

I wasn't entirely sure that was true, but Nisha gave me a small smile as we sat down in the noisy hall.

"Thanks, Ellie," she said quietly.

Poppy didn't reappear until registration. She came in late, looking a bit flustered. She said she'd got lost and had missed lunch, which earned Nisha a questioning look from Miss Dubois. As Poppy took her place next to Nisha, I wondered if I caught the shadow of a smile on her face.

The next day Poppy kept managing to slip away from Nisha and turn up late for lessons, saying she'd got lost. By the time the final bell went, Nisha was getting a few stern looks from teachers and was looking pretty frazzled.

"Come on, Nisha! It's drama club next, it'll be fun!" Lexie said as we walked out of the classroom.

"Yeah, not much can happen there," Jas added.

Nisha looked around to see where Poppy was. Her step-sister was hanging back – she seemed to be doing anything she could to keep her distance from Nisha.

We all went over to remind her about drama club.

"I don't see why I can't just get the bus home. Mum lets me go everywhere alone," Poppy moaned.

"It's only for an hour," Jas said defensively. "You could join in." Poppy gave Jas a mad look, but said nothing. "What? It's fun."

"If it was street dance, I might be tempted," Poppy

53

said, as we trooped through the maze of corridors. "But not drama, that's for geeks."

Kirsty was just behind us. "That's exactly what I say, too," she suddenly piped up, trying to catch Poppy's eye.

Poppy blanked her. "Anyway, I'm just going to get something from my locker," Poppy said. "I'd better get ready for an hour of boredom. At least I've got my iPod."

Kirsty pouted as Poppy fished her iPod out of her bag and popped the headphones on. I could hear the muffled beat of her favourite music as she headed off towards the lockers.

"It's in the main hall! Poppy!" Nisha called out to her. But Poppy kept walking.

"Do you think I should go after her to make sure she doesn't get lost?" Nisha asked anxiously.

"You've told her a zillion times today – she'll find it," Lexie sighed. "Come on, or we'll be late."

In drama we were developing our witches scene and we got so into it that we lost track of time. It wasn't until Poppy suddenly made her entrance at the back of the hall that we noticed she'd been missing. For ages. And she didn't just slip in quietly, either, she came in with a bit of a choking sob.

Mrs Crawfield looked up when she heard the noise, along with the rest of the drama club. She quickly stepped over to Poppy, closely followed by me and my BFFs.

"It's Poppy, isn't it?" Mrs Crawfield asked. Poppy nodded miserably. "What on earth's the matter? And Nisha, I believe you're meant to be buddying Poppy. Why was she wandering around on her own?"

"I was! I have been, I mean." Nisha stumbled over the words, before turning to Poppy. "Where have you been? You only went to the lockers!"

"You didn't tell me which hall drama was in," Poppy sniffed, holding her map. "There's more than one on here and I've been walking round for ages trying to find you!"

Mrs Crawfield called out to the rest of the club, who were looking over at us, to concentrate on their scenes. As the noise picked up again, Mrs Crawfield turned to the four of us. "I will be reporting this to Miss Dubois. I will also ask all the teachers to keep a close eye to ensure that no more mishaps like this occur," Mrs Crawfield said with a voice of steel. "Understood?"

Nisha nodded, biting her lip. Poppy sniffed. Mrs

Crawfield turned her unflinching gaze on to her. "Well, you're here safely now, Poppy. I suggest you sit quietly at the back and use your time wisely. Maybe you could study that map. Girls, back to your scene."

As Poppy turned away, Nisha glanced over at her. She gasped. "Did you see that?" Nisha whispered.

"What?"

"Poppy just smirked! I'm sure of it!"

Lexie looked at her questioningly. "I think your imagination might be working overtime, Nish."

But Nisha looked convinced of what she'd seen and I wondered – could Poppy's entrance have been a performance? Maybe drama wasn't just for geeks, after all...

Trin shares a secret and me and Jas try to fix things...

Miss Dubois called Nisha and Poppy to her desk before registration the next morning. Me, Lexie and Jas sat at our desks, straining to hear the hushed conversation.

"Mrs Crawfield told me what happened at drama club," Miss Dubois said, looking between the two girls. "Nisha, I want to remind you that you're meant to be Poppy's buddy. I appreciate it can be a tricky job when there's lots of things going on, but please try, *oui*?"

"I was!" Nisha replied desperately.

"Sorry, Miss Dubois," Poppy said sweetly, looking at Miss Dubois with big eyes. "I'm sure it was my fault.

57

I mean, I had a map, I just got lost in all the corridors."

Miss Dubois smiled at Poppy and softened for a moment. "Both of you must make an effort, *oui*?" Nisha nodded. "OK, so to your seats, please."

While Nisha and Poppy took their seats, the boys started talking about the big Premier League football match at the weekend.

"It's going to be a top game," Zac boomed. Everything about him was supersized, including his voice. "My dad's going to try and get tickets."

Lexie's ears pricked up. She was really sporty, just like the rest of her family. Her dad and twin brother, Luke, were both mad about football, and Lexie loved it, too. She was always joining in the frequent kickabouts in their back garden, and she was as much of a football expert as any of the boys in our class.

"I'll be going, defo," Jordan replied. "I think we've got a chance of getting higher up the table."

"It'll be a tough game to win, though," Lexie chipped in. "It's the best draw of the season. I'm going with Dad and Luke – I'm really excited about it!"

Poppy glanced up, taking an interest all of a sudden, once Lexie got involved. "Really?" she asked. "My dad loves football. I've been to a few matches with him.

I might ask if he can get us tickets. We could meet up there, Lexie, it'll be fun!"

Nisha's eyes flashed to Lexie, waiting to see what her BFF was going to say. Lexie caught the look, but she was in a really awkward position – I mean, she couldn't just say "no", could she? "Oh, um, maybe," she mumbled.

"I know, why don't we all go?" Nisha suggested quickly.

"But you three don't even like football!" Lexie replied, without thinking.

Poppy raised an eyebrow at Nisha. "No point in Dad buying extra tickets in that case. After all, it's a Premier League match, so they won't be cheap," she said, before smiling at Lexie. "I'm looking forward to it already!"

Some of the boys had been listening. "Might see you there then, Poppy," Tom said bravely, before going crimson.

"Yeah, me, too," Jordan added, as Zac giggled like a girl behind them.

Kirsty looked across, clearly on "boy flirtation alert". Only this time, to her annoyance, it wasn't aimed at her! Kirsty wrinkled her nose. It had clearly been put

out of joint by the attention Poppy was generating.

"*Excuse-moi*, Miss Dubois," Kirsty said, putting up her hand.

"*Qu'est-ce que c'est?*" Miss Dubois asked, opening her register.

"I just wanted to remind everyone about the modelling show. It's in two weeks' time at the Hyper shopping centre," Kirsty said loudly. "I might have already mentioned that I've been asked to be a catwalk model. I said that I'd spread the word at school to make sure everyone comes. That's all."

"This is exciting for you, *non*?" Miss Dubois smiled warmly.

"So exciting," Kirsty replied, lapping up the attention from our form teacher. "In fact, I may even get talent-spotted, who knows?" She smiled, casting a seriously superior look in Poppy's direction. Not that Poppy even noticed.

When we left registration, Nisha looked pretty down. It didn't help when Poppy asked to swap and sit next to Lexie in geography. "So we can talk about where to meet on Saturday and stuff," Poppy said.

"OK then," Nisha said, forcing a smile.

"Don't worry, Nisha. It's only a football match,"

True Colours

I said quietly, as Nisha moved to sit next to Zophia in the spare seat.

"I know," Nisha sighed. "But why would Poppy want to go just with Lexie, if it wasn't to wind me up? It would have been nicer if we could have all gone together, that's all."

After the reminder from Miss Dubois, Nisha made extra efforts to keep her step-sister in sight at all times, which only had the effect of winding up Poppy more. But Nisha's patience started to wear thin as the week went on. Whatever she did, Poppy got more and more impatient with her. But to everyone else, it seemed Poppy was on her best behaviour.

To make matters worse, Nisha thought the teachers were giving Poppy special treatment. It was OK for Poppy to hand in homework that would have got us into trouble for being too short. And she got away with skipping the maths homework completely because she didn't understand the equations. As we started going through the answers, Mr Zyal let Poppy out to go to the loo.

"She just has to smile and make her eyes all big, and

she can get away with anything!" Nisha complained in a whisper.

"But Mr Zyal did say that Poppy was bound to struggle, as they'd covered different topics at her school," Jas pointed out.

"I guess," Nisha sighed, as she put a cross by another answer. "But it still feels a bit unfair."

By Friday lunchtime, Nisha was ready to snap.

"I don't believe this," she said, as she looked round the dining hall. "Poppy's vanished again! She's doing this on purpose!"

"We better get searching," I sighed.

"I've got cross-country," Lexie reminded us.

"In that case, it's just the three of us," Jas said, making an effort to be cheery. "Come on, let's go. See you later, Lexie."

We scoured the dining hall, then the cloakrooms, before we finally – as a last resort – checked the library. And there she was! Trin, Molly, Tabitha and Zophia were all at a table with Poppy. As soon as they saw us, they gave Nisha a cool stare.

"Ah, girls, you're a bit late, but all are welcome at our humble reading group!" Mr Flight beamed at us.

"Oh, no, we didn't mean to interrupt," Nisha said,

as everyone stared at us. "I just wanted to see if Poppy was in here, that's all."

"Ah, yes, the new Miss Harris!" Mr Flight said. "She was wandering the corridors looking a little lost. But luckily Zophia found her and brought her here."

Poppy glanced at the girls on her table, who exchanged knowing looks with each other.

"We'll take Poppy to registration," Molly said to Nisha stiffly. "Don't worry."

"Thanks." Nisha smiled.

"Did anyone else notice Trin and the others' faces?" I asked as we headed down the stairs to the dining hall. "Either they weren't enjoying the reading group, or something else had upset them."

"By the look they gave us as we walked in," Nisha said, in a small voice, "I think that the 'something else' might be me."

Nisha looked really down for the rest of lunch, but she decided that she would invite Poppy to go to the Ace Diner after school to try and smooth things over.

"I think I need to ask her what's going on," Nisha said, "because she clearly doesn't like me, but I haven't got a clue what I've done to upset her."

"Maybe she's just fed up with the whole babysitting

thing?" Jas suggested.

"Well, whatever it is," I said, "I think it's a really good idea to talk to Poppy. If something's bugging her, you can't sort it out unless you know what it is."

It didn't help that, at afternoon registration, Molly sat with Poppy and gave Nisha another cool stare. When the bell rang and the class crowded out of the room to get to PSHE, I decided that I would try to help Nisha. It was obvious that she was feeling really bad, and she hadn't done anything wrong! I pulled Trin to one side in the corridor.

"Is everything OK?" I asked. Trin frowned. "With Poppy, I mean."

"I … I promised I wouldn't say anything," Trin said. "Sorry, Ellie."

Trin turned to walk away. I was about to leave it, but I couldn't because her answer proved that something was definitely wrong.

"Come on, Trin. Please tell me. What if it was one of your best friends in this situation?" I asked her. "You'd want to know what was going on, wouldn't you?"

Trin looked around, quickly checking whether Poppy was there. But she was way up the corridor with Molly and Zophia.

True Colours

"Listen, you didn't hear it from me, but Poppy told us she's avoiding Nisha," she spilled.

"That much is obvious," I said. "But why?"

"She said Nisha's making her feel unwelcome at home," Trin revealed. "She feels like she's in the way all the time and that Nisha can't wait for her to disappear back to London. She's pretty upset about it."

I stopped dead. I knew my BFF had made a huge effort, while Poppy was the one making *Nisha* feel uncomfortable. "But Nisha's gone out of her way to make her feel welcome," I said.

Trin raised a questioning eyebrow. "Well, that's not what Poppy's saying. And Nisha *was* being pretty mean about Poppy before she came to Priory Road – we all overheard her moaning."

"She was just letting off steam," I explained. Although I guess it didn't look like that from Trin's point of view.

"Maybe you should speak to Poppy about it," she suggested. "Then you'll get to hear her side of the story, not just Nisha's."

I mulled over my dilemma all through PSHE – should I tell Nisha what Trin had said, or not? I didn't want to upset her any more, or spark anything off between her

and Poppy. But on the other hand, it felt weird knowing what Poppy was saying behind my BFF's back. I asked Jas during our next lesson, music. In the end we both agreed that it might be best to give Poppy a chance to explain before we said anything to Nisha.

"After all," Jas whispered as Mr Thomas played us a classical music track, "they might just have got their wires crossed. We might be able to help sort it out!"

At break, I clocked Poppy heading for the cloakrooms with Molly, Trin and Tabitha.

"Um, I'm just going to check something in my coat before maths," I said to Lexie and Nisha. "I think I left some money in my pocket."

"I'll come with you," Jas said, bundling after me.

Poppy was sitting with the others, laughing at something Molly had just said.

"Mind if we speak to Poppy for a bit?" Jas asked.

Trin nodded, and they all shuffled up the bench a bit.

Poppy half-smiled at us. "Don't tell me, Nisha sent you to check up on me, right?"

"No, actually, she didn't," Jas corrected her.

"So, what's up then?" Poppy asked, looking between us.

"It's just, we know this whole situation must be pretty weird for you," I said, "but Nisha's our best friend, and she's finding it really difficult, too and—"

"Hang on a second!" Poppy cut me off. She raised her voice, so that Trin and the others could hear. "*Nisha's* finding it difficult?! Is that what you've come to tell me?"

"We just think you should give her a break, that's all. She's trying really hard…" Jas said.

"Give *her* a break?" Poppy almost laughed, but tears sprang to her eyes. "You two are so … so clueless! In case you hadn't noticed, *I'm* the one that's been dumped with Dad in some random house, with virtual strangers. *I'm* the one whose mum is halfway across the world, and whose best friend is miles away. What's *Nisha* got to moan about?"

"Oh, but…" I stuttered.

"Look, just leave it," Poppy said fiercely, getting up and storming out of the cloakroom without a backward glance.

Trin looked at me. Poppy's reaction seemed to confirm everything that Poppy had told them about Nisha. "She's kind of got a point," Molly said, and I began to wonder if they were right. Maybe we hadn't

really thought about everything from Poppy's side. But as they got up to leave, I realized that Poppy had managed to twist everything back to her again, like she was the only one that mattered. She'd neatly side-stepped any explanations for why she was being mean about Nisha behind her back, or taking her problems out on her step-sister.

At that moment the bell rang and we hot-footed it after Poppy. She crashed through the double doors ahead of us and almost ran straight into Nisha and Lexie.

"Oh, hi, Poppy," Nisha started. "I wondered if you fancied going into town tonight after school?"

"With you?" Poppy replied, pushing past. "Not in a million years!

"What's up with her now?" Lexie asked, rolling her eyes. "She's such a drama queen!"

Me and Jas exchanged glances. We'd meant to make things better by talking to Poppy, but instead it looked like we'd just made the situation a thousand times worse.

Lexie delivers some truly REVOLTING news – eurgh!

A whistle blew, echoing around the pool.

"Ellie!"

I suddenly heard my name being called and looked across to see my swimming coach waving crossly at me.

"You're meant to be racing!" he shouted. "Go!"

In the lanes either side of me, the others were already swimming. I flung myself into the pool with a smooth dive and dolphin-kicked my legs like crazy until my head hit the surface and I broke into front crawl. I swam fast, but the late start was too much to make up and I finished in fourth place.

We always finished our swimming sessions with a race. I hadn't been beaten for ages, but tonight my mind was all over the place. I kept thinking about the disastrous conversation Jas and I had had with Poppy earlier.

On the way home in the car, Dad asked me if everything was OK. "You were so distracted tonight, Ellie. What's up?"

"Oh, school stuff," I explained.

"Anything I can help with?" Dad asked.

"It's this situation with Nisha and Poppy," I sighed. "They just aren't getting on. Poppy's upset about being here, but she seems to be taking it out on Nisha and getting her into trouble at school. None of us can work out why."

I explained briefly what had happened, leading up to Poppy's outburst. "And another thing I don't get is why Poppy doesn't want to be at Nisha's house. I thought she'd be happy to spend time with her dad."

"It's a tough one," Dad agreed. "But things can be tricky for children when parents split up. I'm sure Poppy *is* pleased to see Dave, really, but it's not that straightforward, is it? She's got to get to know his whole new family at the same time, too."

True Colours

"I guess," I said, looking out of my window, but that still didn't seem to explain why Poppy was being so off with Nisha.

I went over to see Jas on Saturday morning and told her what Dad had said.

"Well, I think Poppy's pretty lucky," she said, shaking her head. "At least Dave wants to see her. He goes down to London every school holidays and now she's getting to spend time with him whilst she's here. We don't hear from my dad for months at a time!"

We were having a girly pampering session, just the two of us. We had our hair held back with headbands and our faces were covered with gooey honey, banana and yoghurt facemasks that we'd made ourselves. We were meant to be relaxing to let the facemasks work their magic for ten minutes, but Jas wasn't very good at taking it easy – she wouldn't stop fidgeting!

"Anyway, no matter *what's* going on with Poppy," I said, trying to talk without moving my face too much, "there's still no excuse for her making out that Nisha's being mean to her, or for getting Nisha into trouble at school."

Jas checked her watch. "It's time we took these facemasks off, before our faces go mushy!"

Five minutes later, our faces were clean and moisturized. We grabbed some orange juice and sat in the comfy sofa in Jas's living room, chatting about the Valentine's disco. We went through what we were planning to wear. Jas was really looking forward to it, but I couldn't help feeling a bit nervous.

"What if you all get asked to dance and I don't?" I said anxiously.

Jas laughed. "I bet you anything that Ed asks you. It's *so* obvious that he likes you!"

"I don't know which is worse ... *not* being asked, or being asked by Ed!"

"What's wrong with Ed?" Jas giggled. "He could be your boyfriend!"

"He's OK, as boys go," I said, not quite believing that I was talking "boyfriends" like it was even a possibility. "And he looks pretty cool on his skateboard, but that doesn't mean I want to go out with him!"

"Don't worry, Ellie. We'll stick together at the disco. There's no way I'm dancing with *any* of the boys from Priory Road, that's for definite! Come on, let's do our nails!"

72

True Colours

Jas lined up the nail varnishes her mum had lent us so we could choose the colours for our pedicure and manicure. We were just about to start when Nisha texted us both.

Fancy hanging out for a bit? I'm bored...

Come round here 4 nail painting? x Jas texted back.

Yey! C u soon! x

I texted Lexie and asked her to come round after football, too, if she could. "Do you think we should tell Nisha what Trin said?" I asked, as we waited for Nisha to arrive.

Jas nodded. "I'd want to know," she said. "*And* about what Poppy said. I just hope she doesn't get upset with us for talking to Poppy without her, that's all."

As soon as Nisha arrived we started doing our nails. Jas painted Nisha's purple with silver dots.

"I'm so glad we didn't go to the football, after all," Nisha confessed. "I got to spend time with Mum and

Callum on my own, for once. It was lovely!"

"Poppy hasn't got back yet, then?" I asked.

Nisha shook her head. "No. Dave's taking her to the cinema after the match. He asked if I wanted to join them, but I said no. I'm sure Dave thought I was being unfair, but Poppy was in such a bad mood with me yesterday, there was no way I'd have gone."

We blew on our nails and I looked at Jas.

"Um, I think we might know why she was in a bad mood," Jas confessed. We spilled the beans and told Nisha what had happened, starting with what Poppy had told Trin and the others.

"I can't believe Poppy's telling everyone that! It's so not true!" Nisha groaned, sinking back into the sofa. "Whenever I try to make an effort with her, she just blanks me. You saw what she was like when I tried to ask her to the diner yesterday!"

"Well," I said, "that might be because me and Jas had just spoken to her."

"We tried to get her to see things from your point of view," Jas added. "But she was only interested in what it was like for her."

"Mum had a few words with me about the whole 'Poppy Situation' earlier, too," Nisha said. "She wanted to know why I wouldn't go to the cinema. When I told her, she gave me a huge hug and said she'd been finding life with Poppy in the house a bit of a strain, too. She's trying to make sure that neither of us feel left out, but *then* she said that if Poppy's being difficult, *I'm* the one who's got to be mature about it." Nisha's eyes welled up. "Mum and me have always been like best friends, only recently she keeps taking Poppy's side. It … it feels like Poppy's stormed in and turned my life upside down! I thought she'd appreciate me giving up my bed for her, and sleeping on the camp bed, but it's like she thinks she's entitled to it! It even feels like she's trying to steal my BFF!"

"What? Lexie?" Jas frowned.

"When Poppy asked Dave to get tickets for the football match, I heard her telling him about how well she was getting on with Lexie. So Dave called Lexie's dad and arranged for them to sit together at the match." Nisha looked worried just thinking about it, blowing on her nails distractedly. "What if Poppy tells Lexie everything that she's been telling the others, and turns Lexie against me?"

"Don't worry, Nisha. Lexie's your BFF!" Jas said. "And we've invited her over after the football – when

she arrives she'll be able to tell you herself!"

"That's right," I chipped in. "Lexie's only known Poppy for five minutes. I'm sure she won't just forget everything she knows about you after spending one afternoon with Poppy!"

"Has Lexie texted back?" Nisha asked. "What if she's having so much fun hanging out with Poppy that she doesn't want to come?"

Jas looked at me. Lexie hadn't replied to the message yet. We were doing everything we could think of to make Nisha feel better, but it wasn't working.

"She probably hasn't seen it yet," I said. "The match must still be going on…" I gave Nisha a smile, but she looked unconvinced.

At that exact moment, my phone lit up and made the funny barking-dog sound that I had set up as my text message alert.

"See!" I cried triumphantly, and grabbed for the phone, nearly wrecking my new manicure in the process. It occurred to me, as I pressed the button to display the message, that I had no idea what I would say to Nisha if Lexie wasn't coming after all. Luckily, we didn't have to worry about that.

True Colours

See you there in 10 mins. I've got goss! x

Even though Nisha relaxed a bit once she'd heard that Lexie was coming over, she still wasn't her usual self. We tried to take her mind off Poppy by talking about the disco. She joined in the coversation, but her heart just didn't seem in it.

Ten slow minutes crawled by whilst we waited for Lexie to arrive, until finally we heard the doorbell ring. Jas sprang up from the sofa and rushed to answer it, with me and Nisha following behind.

"Ugh, I *had* to get Dad to drop me off straight after the match!" Lexie said as she leaped out of the rain into Jas's tiny hallway. She yanked her wet trainers off and dashed into the living room. Suddenly, the whole room was filled with energy as Lexie plumped down on the beanbag, her eyes shining with excitement. "I have *the* most revolting news to tell you!"

"What?" Jas demanded.

"Poppy only fancies Luke!"

"Noooooooooooo!" we all squealed, laughing into the cushions.

Lexie shuddered. "I mean, he's my brother! And she called him a hottie!"

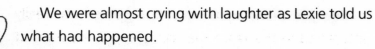

We were almost crying with laughter as Lexie told us what had happened.

"And what makes it a trillion times *more* revolting," Lexie said, "is that Luke actually smiled back at her a few times and said that she's 'all right for a girl'!"

"Noooooo!"

At that moment, Josh walked in. "It's like a witches' coven in here with all this cackling. What's so funny?"

"Luke and Poppy!" Jas gasped.

Josh shook his head. "Girl stuff," he muttered. "I'll leave you to it."

Once we'd recovered from our laughing fits, it was clear Nisha had something on her mind. "So, did you hang out with Poppy much today?"

Lexie screwed up her face. "She kept asking lots of silly questions about football. She clearly hasn't got a clue about it," Lexie explained. "I had to talk to her for a bit – I couldn't ignore her. But as soon as she started going on about Luke, I just felt queasy! I offered to swap seats with her, so she could sit next to him. After that she kept looking in his direction and left me alone – result!"

We giggled again, as Lexie did impressions of them both. "Oh, and guess what else? Poppy said she'd

True Colours

done a bit of cheerleading at school. She was really interested in the team that came out to perform at half-time."

"Ooh, why don't we introduce her to Saskia and Nemone from Peregrine?" Nisha suggested, her face lighting up.

"That's just what I was thinking," Lexie agreed.

"That's an ace idea!" I said. "Their squad meets up on a Tuesday evening in town. Sooo, if Poppy fancied joining them, she wouldn't be hanging around during drama club!"

"Perfect!" Lexie beamed. "Now all we have to do is get her to agree."

"Tell her Luke goes!" I said, setting the others off at the thought of Luke in long socks and a frilly skirt.

"I'm so lucky I've got you three as my BFFs," Nisha said cheerfully. "I really needed a good laugh today!"

We all snuggled down on the sofa under a mound of blankets and watched a DVD while the rain drummed against the windows. When it was time to go, Nisha was still smiling. She seemed the happiest she'd been for ages.

Happiness in Nisha-land doesn't last long while Poppy's in town

"Here's my reply slip for the disco, Miss Dubois!" Kirsty had waited until nearly everyone was at registration on Monday morning before handing it in. She glanced around the class, glowing with excitement. "I'll be so busy that week – it's the fashion show one weekend, then the disco the next!"

Kirsty walked to her desk, fluttering her eyelashes at all the boys on the way. Poppy's presence in class had obviously dented her confidence in the lead-up to Valentine's Day. But whatever she did, it was clear that the boys were still more interested in the new girl. Although now we knew that Poppy wasn't interested in anyone from Kingfisher!

"Are you three going to the disco?" Poppy asked, turning in her chair to face me, Lexie and Jas.

We looked at each other. The junior disco at Christmas had been lots of fun, and there was no way we'd miss the Valentine's disco. But I was a bit embarrassed to be the first to say I wanted to go. I didn't want to sound too eager in front of the whole class. What if all the boys started teasing me? "I guess I will … if you guys do…?" I said hesitantly, waiting for Jas to comment.

But Jas was only half listening. She was concentrating on the fact that Ed was trying to eavesdrop. He was balancing on one leg of his chair, looking out of the window, but leaning in our direction.

"I think someone else is interested in whether you're going or not, too," Jas said loudly. Ed wobbled on his chair and glanced over with an awkward smile. I blushed pink. Sometimes Jas could be so embarrassing!

"Well, I'm going," Lexie announced. "But only if everyone else does…"

"I'm in," Jas agreed, still grinning.

Nisha reached into her bag. "You better come, because I've got mine and Poppy's reply slips here." Nisha smiled, but Poppy looked straight through her. Her shoulders slumped as she took the slips to the front.

While Nisha was away from the desk, Poppy turned to Lexie. "So, do you think your brother will go?" she asked casually.

"Um, maybe," Lexie said. Jas and me looked away and pretended we didn't know anything about Poppy's crush. "I can ask him for you if you like?"

"Oh, no." Poppy blushed faintly. "I was just wondering, that's all."

"He's got a football match the day after, for his league club," Lexie said. "So he wasn't sure about going. The local cheerleading team are going to perform for the first time. Did Nisha tell you about the cheerleading club?"

"No, she didn't," Poppy said, just as Nisha came back to her seat. Poppy turned her head away, avoiding Nisha's eyes.

"I did!" Nisha replied indignantly. "Before dinner, yesterday."

Poppy made her wide-eyed and innocent face.

82

True Colours

"I don't remember."

Lexie moved swiftly on. "Anyway, you know you said you did cheerleading at your school?"

"A bit." Poppy nodded.

"Well, we've got a couple of friends in Peregrine – Saskia and Nemone. They're in the cheerleading club. They practise every Tuesday after school. We wondered if you'd like to meet them."

"Are Saskia and Nemone going to be part of the cheerleading group performing at the football match?" Poppy asked. Lexie nodded. "I might as well give it a go – sounds like it might be fun! Thanks, Lexie!"

We found Saskia and Nemone by the lockers before geography. Lexie introduced them to Poppy and they arranged to meet up at lunchtime to talk cheerleading. After listening to Mr "Wiggy" Wigglesworth, our rock-obsessed geography teacher, witter on for ages about sediment, we were released for lunch. Saskia and Nemone were already in the dining hall and they waved Poppy over to their table.

"Maybe if Poppy finds something she enjoys she'll

settle in a bit more," I suggested.

"I hope so," Nisha agreed.

"Until then, I guess you'll just have to stick it out," Lexie said. "I mean, she can't stay forever, can she?"

Maybe that wasn't the best thing to say. The thought of Poppy never leaving must have freaked Nisha out, because she gasped and began to choke on her sandwich! Lexie thwacked her on the back several times, as tears streamed down her face.

"Are you OK?" Tabitha asked. A group of girls crowded round, trying to help. Nisha coughed and spluttered, as Lexie hit her on the back again until she finally started to recover. There was only one person who didn't seem to care at all, sitting with her back firmly to Nisha, and that was Poppy.

The next day Nisha came into registration at the very last minute, just as Miss Dubois was closing the door. She walked to her chair with her head down, but I could see that her eyes were all red and puffy.

"What's up?" I whispered to her, as Miss Dubois started taking the register.

"I'm fine," Nisha said, forcing a smile and

84

pretending to look for something in her bag. But her wobbling chin gave away how she really felt.

She stayed quiet all day. Lexie, Jas and me took it in turns to quiz her, but she kept insisting that nothing was the matter. Even in art she just kept herself to herself. She frowned, staring at her design and sighing. Then she put it to one side and started on a new one.

Miss Malik noticed Nisha's downbeat mood. "Nisha, are you finding this difficult?" she asked gently, as Nisha screwed up yet another piece of paper.

"I ... I just don't think it's working," Nisha said.

Miss Malik frowned. "Show me," she said, leaning over to take a look.

Nisha reluctantly pulled out her first design. "It's just really boring," Nisha said quietly.

"I think it's original," Miss Malik disagreed. "And very you." Nisha rolled her eyes at that. "Come on, stick with it, it's really starting to take shape. OK?"

Nisha nodded, but she didn't look convinced.

When the final bell went, Poppy rushed off to meet Saskia and Nemone. Saskia's mum Cheryl had spoken to Dave about the arrangements. Poppy was going to get the bus with her new friends, and Cheryl would pick her up afterwards and drop her home. But even

Poppy's absence during drama club didn't lift Nisha's spirits.

Nisha didn't lighten up all week. In fact, she just got even quieter and nothing that we said seemed to cheer her up. Then, in physics on Friday, she did something totally out of character. When Mr Temple asked for our homework, Poppy told him that she hadn't done hers. At first she was reluctant to tell him why, but finally she said that it was because Nisha hadn't let her share the textbook. Mr Temple called Nisha to his desk and proceeded to ask why she had "purposely withheld" her textbook. Nisha just blew.

"I did not!" she raged. "Poppy's lying! She's trying to land me in trouble on purpose – she's trying to ruin everything I do! I know she is!"

Mr Temple sent her straight into lunchtime detention with our fierce deputy head and history teacher, Mr Wood.

"This whole thing between Nisha and Poppy has spiralled way out of control," Lexie said, as we sat in the dining hall, waiting for her to come out.

We all agreed that there was no way Nisha would

True Colours

have kept her textbook from Poppy, however annoying she was being. Poppy must have been lying.

"But it's so unlike Nisha to fly off the handle like that," I said.

"Exactly – Nisha's put up with lots from Poppy so far," Jas agreed, "so why suddenly blow now?"

I checked my watch, then looked up to see if there was any sign of Nisha. "Don't you think she's been acting a bit strangely all week? I reckon something's happened that Nisha hasn't told us about."

"Well, now's our chance to find out," Lexie said, as Nisha appeared, looking totally downcast.

Nisha 'fesses up, but it doesn't help much

We collared Nisha when she appeared in the dining hall after her detention. We knew that she wouldn't tell us anything with everyone around having lunch, so we dragged her outside for a chat. We pulled on our coats, braved the chilly playground and sat at one of the benches. Our breath came out in great white plumes.

"Listen, Nisha," Lexie began, "we wanted to talk to you before lessons start. We need you to tell us what's up. Even if Poppy lied about her homework to try and get you into trouble, it's so not like you to flip out like that."

"What's changed suddenly?" I asked.

True Colours

Tears welled up in Nisha's eyes and rolled down her cheeks as she sat silently and shook her head. "I … I can't say."

"But we're your BFFs, Nisha," Jas said, "you can tell us anything."

Nisha sighed heavily, looking at the floor.

"Nothing can be that bad," I reassured her.

"Well…" Nisha began hesitantly. "Promise you won't tell?"

"Promise," we all said.

"The thing is, I … I read one of Poppy's emails." She looked up and registered our shocked faces. "I didn't mean to, it … it just kind of happened…"

I glanced at the other three. "How?"

"She left the laptop open, with a half-written email on the screen," Nisha explained. "I went to use it and … I couldn't help reading."

"So what did it say?" Lexie asked.

"It was to her best friend, Angel. It started off saying that she really missed London and that she wished she could have stayed with Angel, not come here, stuff like that…" Nisha looked at us and carried on. "Then she said that this was a 'backwater', and that life with me was 'really boring'." Nisha sniffed. "She reckoned we

have nothing in common because I was a 'goody two-shoes', and that she wanted to mess up my so-called 'perfect' life – at school and at home. I was *sure* she was faking it when she was getting lost all the time and acting really upset, and now I know she was. That's how I know she landed me in trouble on purpose today!"

I fished around in my bag for a tissue and passed it to Nisha. "Is that what you were upset about when you came into school on Tuesday morning?"

Nisha nodded miserably. "But I've never tried to pretend that my life's perfect. I don't get why she would even think that." Nisha twizzled the tissue through her fingers. "Do … do you all think I'm boring, too?"

"No!" we chorused.

"Poppy doesn't know what she's talking about!" Lexie added, making Nisha's tears well up again.

"You're thoughtful and caring," I said, putting my arm round her shoulders. "That's *not* boring!"

"So, what should I do?" Nisha sniffed.

"I reckon we should talk to Poppy tonight," Lexie said. "She's completely out of order!"

"We can hardly come straight out with it," I said.

"Not when Nisha shouldn't have read the email in the first place."

"At least now I know why my efforts at making friends with Poppy fell so flat," Nisha said, wiping her nose. The bell rang and we all got up to go back in for registration.

"Well, it's the weekend tomorrow," I said. "If you want to steer clear of Poppy you could always come round to mine?"

"I wish I could," Nisha said, "but I've got to spend the whole day with Poppy! Dave's busy with this big project and he's been working late to catch up after the week he took off when Poppy arrived. Tomorrow is the first day he's managed to get off since then and he and Mum have organized a family day out. We're going to go out for a walk and a meal, or something like that. They said it should help me and Poppy 'bond'..."

The four of us looked at each other and, despite everything, we started to giggle.

As we got to our classroom for registration, I slumped into my seat. I felt exhausted. "What a week! I can't wait for a lie-in tomorrow," I said to Jas. "I could so do without swimming club tonight!"

"I don't suppose you fancy going to the cinema tomorrow, do you?" Jas asked. "Lexie's going to one of Luke's football matches, Nisha's going to be busy all day – that just leaves us!"

"Sounds like a plan," I said.

Our conversation was interrupted by the sound of the classroom door swinging open and banging against the wall. Kirsty had clearly decided to make a big entrance and she wanted everyone to know about it. She stalked in with her chin up, swinging her hips in a really OTT way.

"Has she forgotten how to walk properly?" Lexie whispered a bit too loudly. Kirsty heard her.

"It's how all the catwalk models walk," Kirsty tutted. "I'm practising for—"

"The fashion show," Jas finished. "We know!"

Everyone giggled, and the laughter didn't stop until Miss Dubois walked into the room and called for silence.

"That was hysterical!" Jas giggled, as we came out of the cinema on Saturday and headed for the bus stop.

"Yeah, hysterically *bad*!" I laughed. We'd just been

to see *Titans of Doom* and it was the worst film ever.

"It was so funny – for all the wrong reasons!" Jas added, wiping her eyes and giggling again.

We'd just got to the bus stop when we saw Nisha on the other side of the road. She was looking fed up, trailing after her mum, who had her hands full with Callum. Poppy was just behind, linking arms with Dave.

"Nisha!" Jas shouted. "Woo-hoo!"

Nisha looked up and broke into a huge grin. They all crossed over and Nisha gave us both a big hug.

"So, where have you been?" I asked, seeing them all wrapped up against the winter chill.

"We went to Ashurst Manor Park," Nisha explained. "It's just outside town. It was amazing! There were deer, antelope and even some zebras there – so cute!"

"So dreary more like," Poppy mumbled under her breath, just loud enough for Nisha to hear, but not Mr and Mrs Harris, who'd just retraced their steps to look for Callum's glove.

"Well, I enjoyed it anyway," Nisha said quietly.

"That's because you don't know what real entertainment is," Poppy added. "You should try living in London for a bit, then you'd know what I mean."

"There is life outside London," Jas replied, just as

Jamila and Dave rejoined us. They noticed the tense atmosphere at once.

"I'm glad we've bumped into you, girls. Do you fancy doing something together tomorrow?" Dave asked. "With Lexie, too, of course. Jamila's going to be busy with Callum and it'll give me time to catch up on a bit of work."

Poppy's face fell. She stared at the ground, but she didn't say anything, just fiddled with the cuff on her coat.

"Um, OK," I agreed, nudging Jas, who nodded. "What does anyone fancy doing?"

"Poppy, is there anything you'd like to try?" Mrs Harris asked.

"There's not exactly a lot to choose from round here, is there?" Poppy said grumpily.

"What about rollerblading?" Jas suggested. "There's a new rink that's just opened. We haven't been yet – maybe we could try it."

"Whatever," Poppy shrugged.

After we made arrangements for the next day, Nisha and her family went off for a pizza in town. Me and Jas got on the bus and flopped on to the nearest seat.

"Well, tomorrow's going to be fun, isn't it?" Jas

groaned. "I think I might have some geography homework I'd rather be doing!"

"I can see the headline now," I joked. "'Fireworks at new rollerblade rink!'"

As it turned out, I wasn't far wrong!

Colourful lights flashed and music blared out, as people spun round the packed rollerblade dance floor. It was so busy that we had to queue for a while to pick up our blades. Poppy had been in a grump from the moment Dave had dropped her and Nisha off, and the hanging around wasn't helping.

"Me and Angel go rollerblading in Hyde Park," she huffed. "We don't just spin round in circles like we're stuck in some goldfish bowl."

When we finally got on the floor, Poppy cheered up a bit – she seemed to enjoy showing off her moves where everyone could watch her. She *was* really good – she could go backwards and do little hops, too. Lexie was a natural. It wasn't long before she was spinning round all over the place. Jas went for it, but it was her legs and arms that went spinning in all directions. Me and Nisha were pretty hopeless, but it

was still fun trying.

We stayed for quite a while and around lunchtime the crowds started to thin.

"Shall we get something to eat?" Lexie asked me and Nisha. As if on cue, her stomach let out the hugest gurgle ever.

"Just a bit longer," Nisha said, looking at Poppy, who was still racing about, enjoying herself. We wobbled round for a few more minutes until Jas dashed past us, totally out of control, heading full pelt for the exit gap.

"I can't turn!" she squealed, grabbing on to me and Nisha as she came past, knocking us both flying. I grabbed the side rail and just managed to stay upright, but Nisha ended up in the middle of the rink, almost doing the splits. Me and Lexie tried to help her up, but we kept slipping, too, and we were laughing too much to keep steady. Poppy bladed past, but she didn't join in with our laughter *or* try to help. Instead she just smirked as she looked down at Nisha on the floor.

Nisha stopped smiling at once. As she got to her feet, she looked really upset. "Right, that's enough," she said. "I can't take this!"

True Colours

Me, Lexie and Jas exchanged glances as Nisha skated up to Poppy, who was taking a break by the side.

"Poppy, what have I done wrong? I don't understand!" she said, trying to control the wobble in her voice.

Poppy shook her head. "You just don't get it, do you?" She rollered straight up to the exit, dragged off her blades, and stormed over to collect her shoes.

"I take it that's the end of rollerblading then," Lexie said.

I wheeled over to where Nisha was still standing, at the edge of the rink. "Are you OK?" I asked. She shook her head and a tear rolled off the end of her nose. "I don't understand what I've done to make Poppy hate me so much! If she won't tell me, I can't do anything about it."

As Jas and Lexie joined us I looked over at Poppy, who was sitting grumpily near the exit. I had no clue why, either, but one thing was clear: Right now, Poppy and Nisha looked as miserable as each other.

Poppy + concert does NOT = happiness!

After our disastrous rollerblade outing, Nisha gave up trying to make friends with her step-sister and decided to ignore her, instead. At least in art she could put her head down and lose herself in her work. It looked like she'd got over her confidence crisis of the week before and all her effort was starting to really pay off. Miss Malik walked around the room, checking our progress one by one. She gave helpful hints about material choices, and how best to show off our designs in the sketches.

"Zac, there appears to be a lack of material samples on your portfolio," Miss Malik observed as she stood beside him. "In fact, there appears to be an overall lack of design. Please explain."

"I'm designing shorts, miss," Zac explained.

"That's all?" Miss Malik questioned.

"Yeah, just shorts."

"Remember the brief, everyone," Miss Malik called out to the class. "It is to design an *outfit* for a fashion show. That outfit could be a full-length garment, or a two-piece, along with shoes and accessories. It cannot, Zac, consist of just a pair of shorts. Ah, Nisha, let me borrow yours for a moment."

Nisha flushed slightly as she handed Miss Malik her portfolio. Our teacher held it aloft and flipped through it, so that we could all see. Nisha had detailed sketches, building up from an idea to a more detailed design, complete with material swatches.

"This, everyone, is what I'm expecting you to produce from the brief I gave you," Miss Malik announced, before giving the artwork back to Nisha. "Well done, this is looking very strong, Nisha."

As Miss Malik walked away, I heard Poppy mutter, "Such a teacher's pet."

Nisha kept her eyes on her work, but I could tell by the way her hands shook slightly that she'd heard Poppy's comment. She wasn't the only one, either.

I caught Trin, Molly and Zophia exchanging surprised glances. I wondered for a second what Nisha was going to do, but she kept her cool.

When the lesson finally ended we were able to ask Nisha about it.

"I can't believe that Poppy said that!" Jas said. "I mean, if it were me, I would have gone crazy at her! Who does she even think she is?"

"It's Dad's gig tomorrow night," Nisha explained, as we wandered along the corridor towards the lockers. "I'm not going to let anything ruin it! It's just going to be me and Mum. Callum's going to his best friend's for the night and Dave's staying in with Poppy. If I get into trouble now, it would be a disaster. I wanted to say something, believe me!"

As we got to the lockers I noticed that Poppy was just behind us. I felt myself blush, wondering how much she had heard.

The next morning in registration, the stand-off between the step-sisters was more tense than ever.

"What's up?" Jas asked Nisha, before Poppy sat down.

True Colours

"Dave's working tonight," Nisha said, fuming. "He's got to take a client for dinner. He was meant to go during the week Poppy was first up here, but he put it off. Now, apparently, tonight's the only time the client can do."

"Does that mean you can't go to the concert?" I asked.

"Oh, we're still going," Nisha explained, as Poppy came over and sat down. "But Poppy has to come with us, that's all."

"Believe me, I'd rather not be coming to see your dad's band," Poppy said loudly. Her mood looked as black as Nisha's.

"You don't need to tell everyone," Nisha said, as a few of the others in the room looked over.

"Your dad's in a band, Nisha?" Travis asked. "You never said."

"No, *I* wouldn't, either!" Poppy laughed. "The band's called The Storm Chasers. That pretty much says it all. Total cringe time. They're so far from cool, they've come out the other side."

Nisha glanced round, biting her lip. Everyone was looking over now, and I worried for a second that they were going to start laughing along with Poppy.

But instead of joining in her so-called joke, Travis looked in awe at Nisha. "That is so cool."

"I'd love *my* dad to be in a band!" Ajay said, grinning. "Does he play lots of shows? Do they have a tour bus?"

Nisha nodded, allowing herself to get a tiny bit excited. "They're on tour most of the time."

"I can't believe you kept that to yourself," Molly said. "I'd tell anyone who'd listen!"

Suddenly everyone was talking about the fact that Nisha's dad was in a band. Poppy shook her head in disgust. "Doesn't *anyone* round here have any taste in music?"

The next second Miss Dubois came in and asked what all the fuss was about. As Nisha shyly told her, Poppy looked like she'd swallowed a wasp.

At lunchtime, Poppy disappeared. She wasn't sitting with Saskia and Nemone, or with Molly and her friends.

Nisha scanned the room anxiously. "I wonder where Poppy is. She hasn't come into the dining hall all lunch…"

"Enjoy the peace while it lasts," Jas joked.

True Colours

But when Poppy didn't show up at registration, the four of us started to get a bit worried.

"Do you think she's OK?" Nisha asked. She was trying hard not to, but she couldn't stop herself being concerned. Just then, Miss Dubois asked to speak to Nisha. She stepped up to the front.

"Poppy's not feeling very well at all," Miss Dubois told her quietly. "She came to the sick bay at lunchtime and we've called your mum to come and pick her up."

"Poppy looked fine earlier, didn't she?" Lexie said, as we headed to afternoon lessons.

Suddenly, Nisha gasped. "I've just thought!" she cried. "Dave's working tonight – so what happens if Poppy's too ill to go to the gig?"

"I'm sure your mum will sort something out," I said. But I could tell by Jas's face that she was wondering the same thing as me. Could Poppy really be mean enough to fake this? I hated to say it, but after the way she'd behaved recently, I was pretty sure that the answer to that was a big, fat yes.

Nisha bit her nails all through the afternoon. At long last, the bell went and she flew out of the school gates. As we raced after her, we saw Mrs Harris's car waiting.

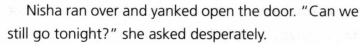

Nisha ran over and yanked open the door. "Can we still go tonight?" she asked desperately.

Nisha's mum looked stressed. "It might be best to talk about it on the way home," she said, clocking me, Lexie and Jas huddled up behind Nisha.

"Please, Mum, just tell me we can still go?"

Jamila sighed heavily. "Dave's tried, but he can't get out of meeting this client tonight, not after cancelling last time," she explained. "And Poppy feels so ill, she needs to be in bed. I really can't leave her with anyone else in this state. I'm so sorry, Nisha."

"I can't believe it!" Nisha gasped. "She's ruining everything!"

"Nisha," Jamila said firmly. "That's enough. I know how disappointing this is for you, but Poppy really can't help being ill."

"She's not ill!" Nisha cried. "She's done this on purpose – she knew how important tonight was for me and she's trying to ruin everything! I know it!"

"Nisha!" Jamila said, sounding shocked. "Why would you think that?"

Nisha opened her mouth, then closed it again. She couldn't spill the secret about the email to her mum, so she did the only thing she could – keep quiet.

True Colours

Jamila sighed, sounding thoroughly fed up. "Come on, I've had enough of this. In the car. We have to get back before Dave leaves."

Nisha got into the car, tears rolling freely down her face now that her anger had subsided. She didn't even look at us as we waved goodbye.

A sticky situation in art makes Nisha SNAP!

The next day Nisha was still fuming about missing the gig. Her mood was made fouler by the fact that Poppy had made what she called a "miraculous" recovery. Apparently Poppy had stopped feeling really sick in the evening and had even managed to have some dinner. She was so much better, in fact, that she'd even made it into school.

Nisha angrily moved her chair away as Poppy sat down in registration.

Poppy rolled her eyes. "I don't get what the big deal is, anyway," she said. "Your dad only lives a few miles away. You must get to see him all the time."

True Colours

Nisha turned on her. "For your information," she said through gritted teeth, "my dad's away touring nearly all the time. I'm lucky if I get to see him twice or three times a year. It's going to be months before I get a chance to see him again. *That's* what the big deal about last night was!"

Nisha turned her back on Poppy. I could see her shaking, and angry tears glistened in her eyes. Poppy sat there silently, stunned by Nisha's response. She was about to say something when the bell went and Nisha stood up and marched out ahead of all of us.

We had art before lunch and Nisha worked like a demon. While the rest of the class were still struggling to get the final designs right, by the time the lesson was almost over, Nisha had finished mounting her work on to a large pasteboard. All the stages of her designs were there, carefully sketched and coloured. It looked incredible, just like the fashion paste-ups Miss Malik had shown us at the start of the project.

Even Kirsty looked impressed. "Maybe when I'm a famous model, after this weekend," she said, wrinkling her nose, "you could do designs for me!"

Everyone around the room groaned at yet another plug for the fashion show. Except for Poppy. She

appeared to be totally absorbed in her work, but when I looked across, I noticed that she was spending ages over tiny details, and not really getting anywhere. She drew over the necklace in her design a hundred times. As she leaned over her page, I noticed that it matched the heart-locket necklace she always wore. It had slipped from inside her T-shirt and was hanging down near the paper.

"Can everyone start to clear up now, please?" called Miss Malik.

Poppy sighed, then got up and carried her unfinished pasteboard over to the racks. She walked past Nisha, who had just stood hers against the bench to let it dry.

"That looks amazing, Nisha," Poppy said sheepishly, but Nisha pretended not to have heard. Poppy hesitated – for a second she looked as if she was trying to find the right words – then she turned round to leave. As she did so, the pasteboard she was holding under her arm knocked a big tub of gooey paste that was sitting on the edge of the bench. It teetered and toppled over.

"Nisha! Look out!" I could see what was about to happen, but I couldn't stop it. Lexie and Molly were both nearer and they grabbed for the tub, but it was too late. It hit Nisha's board, spewing paste, which slowly slid down over the designs.

"No!" Nisha cried, grabbing for a cloth and dabbing at the dripping paste. Lexie and Molly tried to help.

"Leave it, girls," Miss Malik said, rushing over and moving them back. "It's best to let it dry. If you try to wipe it now it'll make everything worse."

"Look at it! It's totally wrecked!" Nisha cried, chucking the cloth down and staring at her work. The material was dripping and some of the artwork was smeared.

Poppy was standing frozen on the spot, her hand over her mouth, aghast. "I'm so sorry!" she began. "I—"

"Sorry?" Nisha turned on her at once. "You're not sorry in the slightest!"

"Nisha, that's enough!" Miss Malik said, looking surprised at Nisha's outburst, as everyone craned to watch.

"It was an accident, I promise!" Poppy insisted.

"Do you expect me to believe that? After everything you've done?" All Nisha's pent-up frustration finally spilled out. "You've messed everything up since you got

here – I wish you'd never come!"

"Catfight!" Zac called out, and some of the boys laughed.

"Quiet, everyone!" Miss Malik insisted as the bell rang. As the rest of the class started to make their escape, Miss Malik turned to Nisha and Poppy. "Now, this is completely unacceptable. Tell me, what's going on here?"

Both the girls stood side by side. Poppy bit her lip, and Nisha stood sullenly silent.

"Right, well if you won't tell me," Miss Malik said, "you can explain everything to Miss Dubois instead. Come with me, please, girls."

With that Miss Malik marched Nisha and Poppy from the art room.

"Wow!" Trin shook her head as we put our work away. "I have never seen Nisha like that, *ever!*"

"It did look like an accident, though," Zophia said, leaving the room ahead of me and Jas.

Molly didn't look convinced. "Maybe, but Poppy *has* been pretty mean to Nisha in the last few days."

Me, Lexie and Jas talked about Nisha's flip as we waited for her to reappear. Jas and Lexie were convinced that Poppy spilled the tub of paste on purpose.

True Colours

"I'm not sure," I said, "I think maybe it was an accident."

"I can't believe you'd take her side," Jas said, giving me a look. "Not after everything she's done to Nisha recently."

Lexie tutted, too. I could see that I wasn't going to convince either of them. I still wasn't a hundred per cent sure, either, but Poppy had seemed subdued. She'd even attempted to be nice to Nisha, which was way out of character.

When Nisha got back she didn't want to talk to us about what Miss Dubois had said, but she was distracted for the rest of the afternoon. As soon as the bell went, we grabbed our coats and headed to the bus stop. Jas tried to cheer Nisha up by chatting away, but she was in a world of her own. I remember how nervous I'd been about going home after I'd got into trouble last term. I whispered "good luck" to Nisha and she headed off to get her bus with Poppy and Lexie.

"Grounded?" Lexie gasped, when Nisha turned up at school the next day. Nisha nodded miserably.

"I've never been grounded before," she sighed.

"Ever. I tried to tell Miss Dubois what was going on, but she insisted on calling Mum to discuss the 'issues' me and Poppy have been having. Poppy kept saying that she had spilled the glue by accident and it ended up sounding like I'd ripped into her for no apparent reason!"

I couldn't decide whether to say what I was thinking or not. For half a second I wavered, then I decided to go ahead. "Well, what if it really was an accident?" I asked, as we walked to our form room.

"Ellie, I thought you were meant to be *my* friend, not *hers*!" Nisha said, looking hurt.

"I am, Nish," I said, "but Poppy looked genuinely upset. I know she's been really nasty, but maybe this time it was an accident...?"

"I know what I read in that email," Nisha replied stiffly. "She did it on purpose."

"What did your mum and Dave say?" Jas asked, swiftly steering Nisha away from my "innocent Poppy" idea.

"They were disappointed," Nisha sighed, "which was kind of worse than them being cross. Mum told me to 'step into Poppy's shoes'. I said fine, but what about anyone stepping into mine for a change?

True Colours

Everyone keeps forgetting that bit." Nisha looked pointedly at me. "Anyway, there's one benefit of still being stuck with the camp bed – I can move it wherever I like. So I've moved it into Callum's room. At least I can escape her for a bit in there."

"So, you're grounded *this* weekend?" Lexie asked. Nisha nodded.

"You're going to miss the event of the year!" Jas said. "No! The event of the CENTURY!"

We all frowned.

"What are you talking about, Jas?!" I asked.

"The catwalk show!" Jas reminded us with a giggle.

"Oooh, are you all coming?" Kirsty was already in the classroom, and overheard the end of our conversation.

"I can't," Nisha sighed.

"But the rest of us will be there," I said. I didn't want to say as much in front of Nisha, but I was looking forward to it. I wasn't fashion-obsessed like Kirsty, but it was going to be fun to see all the different clothes. Miss Dubois wished Kirsty luck, and asked who was going. Most of the class were planning to and everyone started chatting away. I looked round and noticed that Poppy was playing with her necklace,

twiddling the locket in her fingers. She was the only person not smiling.

Kirsty rules the catwalk and Nisha regrets something she DOESN'T do...

There were lots of people milling around at the shopping centre. Mum and Dad needed to do some shopping, so I went in with them. We had breakfast in one of the big department stores as a treat. After I'd finished my blueberry muffin and hot chocolate, I went to meet up with Jas and Lexie. The catwalk for the fashion show had been set up near Miss Butterfly, one of our favourite clothes shops. It was mid-morning and passers-by were beginning to stop as the loudspeaker crackled into life. There were quite a few people from school there – including Ed and Zac!

"Come to get some fashion tips?" Jas called out.

"It's Zac that needs them, not me!" Ed joked back, earning a thwack from his mate.

Zophia came over and stood with us, along with Molly, Trin and Tabitha. They were going to the cinema after the fashion show. Saskia and Nemone were there, too, and we spotted some Year Nines and Tens in the crowd.

Music started thumping out over the loudspeakers and the models appeared and lined up, ready to strut their stuff. I noticed Dave and Poppy wandering through the crowds. Dave pointed us out to Poppy and I half-waved, before Jas poked me hard in the ribs with her elbow.

"Look!" she cried. "It's Kirsty!"

Kirsty marched down the catwalk like a thing possessed, her hips swinging wildly, her eyes fixed and her face stony, just like she'd practised at school. Next to her was her best friend, Eliza, doing the same.

"They look like demented twins!" I gasped.

That sent Jas and Lexie into hysterics. Just behind them Amelia from Year Ten glided down the catwalk elegantly, stopping to pose at the end with a brief smile before turning and following Kirsty and Eliza off. The older boys went wild, whooping and whistling. Kirsty and Eliza tilted their noses a little higher, and gave a small smile to each other as they left the catwalk.

"Kirsty *so* thought that cheering was for her!" Molly giggled.

I noticed Poppy say something to Dave, then make her way through the crowds towards us. She looked awkward and her eyes had dark shadows under them. I smiled, but noticed that Lexie and Jas both had stony faces that were not very different from Kirsty's model expression.

"Hi," Poppy said quietly.

"Hi," I said, and glared at the other two, who both reluctantly said hello.

"Look, I really wanted to talk to you about—"

At the same moment Kirsty tottered over and barged right in, still in her catwalk outfit. "OMG – did you *hear* the football team go wild when I was on the catwalk?" she gushed, checking to see who was looking over at her. For once she was actually smiling.

Poppy gave a heavy sigh, then turned away.

"What's up with her?" Kirsty demanded, frowning. She had clearly forgotten all her rules about face composure for minimal wrinkles in the excitement. "Jealous, no doubt. I bet she's never done anything this

amazing, even in London!"

Kirsty turned on her heel, craning her neck to see who else she could show off to.

"Poppy!" I called out. But she'd disappeared back into the crowds. Eventually I spotted her and Dave heading in the direction of the car park. He had his arm round her shoulders.

"I wonder what she wanted?" Jas asked suspiciously.

"I guess we'll never know," I sighed, "thanks to supermodel Kirsty."

"You should have heard them go crazy!" Kirsty must have repeated her modelling story about a thousand times before Miss Dubois even stepped into the room on Monday morning. She was sitting with Trin, Molly and Zophia, who had made the mistake of asking her one question about it. They looked like they wished they hadn't as Kirsty went on, and on, and on... "And Mum and Dad bought me the modelling outfit, in case I want to wear it to the Valentine's disco this Friday. I haven't decided if I will yet, though – I might want a fresh look. Do you know what I mean?"

True Colours

I tried to ignore Kirsty's hysteria as we caught up with Nisha to find out how her weekend had been.

"It was all right, really," she said quietly. "I did my homework, and helped Mum with Callum. Mum made me tidy my room while Poppy was out, even though I'm not sleeping in there at the moment! The weird thing was," she said, dropping her voice even more, "that when Poppy got back she actually said thanks! Like I was doing it for her!"

"Maybe she was trying to make up with you?" I suggested.

"I don't care if she was," Nisha said.

I raised an eyebrow. Over the last week, Nisha really hadn't been acting like her usual self. She must have got my look, because she blushed slightly as the bell went and we headed for PE.

Over the next couple of days there was a buzz growing around the bustling corridors at Priory Road. Valentine's Day always used to pass us by at Woodview, our primary school, but here it was a major event, and the disco was even more of a big deal. Kirsty and Eliza were behaving as though

getting Valentine's cards was an Olympic sport – and they were going for gold. It required a huge amount of hair flicking and eyelash fluttering and they spent every spare second planning their outfits for the disco. They were sketching different combinations on big pieces of paper, just like we were in art. Miss Malik would have been proud.

But Kirsty and Eliza weren't the only ones to be struck by Valentine fever. There were lots of whispered conversations in friendship huddles during break and lunchtimes. Jas kept winding me up, telling me that Ed was looking over and Zac would make kissing noises when I walked past him and Ed. I spent most of the week as pink as a shrimp, telling Jas off and scowling at Zac. I was worried that all Jas's nudges were going to give Ed the wrong impression! The only people not enjoying the Valentine build-up were Nisha and Poppy, who were both still as glum as the constant rain outside.

On Wednesday afternoon the weather got even worse. As we got changed for PE after break no one wanted to go outside. We could see through the window that it was pouring with rain. The trees were being buffeted by gusty winds and it was freezing. Running around chasing a hockey ball was seriously uninviting.

Eventually, Terrifying Townsend, our PE teacher, got fed up waiting for us to come out on to the pitch and charged in to find out what the delay was. "Come on!" she roared as she strode in. "A bit of rain won't hurt you! We've got a match to play. Get moving, everyone!"

We all groaned. I was on a total go-slow and Jas had managed to put on her tracksuit bottoms the wrong way round.

"Come on, guys," Lexie said, trying to chivvy us along. Ever since she had been put into the cross-country and netball teams, she'd tried to keep on Terrifying Townsend's good side.

"I'm coming – hang on," Jas said, wriggling out of her tracksuit and almost falling in a heap.

Soon we were the only ones left in the changing rooms, along with Kirsty. She always had to check her appearance in the mirror before leaving.

"Oooh, what's that? A necklace!" Kirsty peered under a bench as she headed to the door. "It doesn't look like anything special," she said, wrinkling her nose.

"It looks a bit like Poppy's," Nisha added, just as the door slammed open.

"Will you lot get out here now!" Terrifying Townsend roared. Nisha hesitated for a second. "NOW!"

Nisha glanced once more at the necklace, but Jas grabbed her arm. "Come on, let's go!" Pulling us with her, she scooted out of the door into the gloomy afternoon.

When I got home that evening, I had a text from Nisha.

Remember that necklace in PE? It WAS Poppy's. She's just realized she lost it. What should I do??

I texted back straight away. **Don't worry. Just tell her where u saw it. U can go and look 4 it first thing 2mrw. x**

OK. Wish me luck! x

I went upstairs to my bedroom to do my homework.

True Colours

We didn't have that much to do, but I ended up sitting there for ages. My mind kept wandering back to Poppy's necklace. She was always fiddling with it and it seemed like it was important to her. I couldn't help worrying about what would happen. What if Poppy thought that Nisha had seen it and left it there on purpose?

By the time Mum called me down for dinner, I had finally managed to get through the maths equations we had been set.

"Coming!" I yelled. I decided to text Nisha quickly, to find out what had happened.

Is everything OK? What did Poppy say?

"Ellie, we're waiting for you! Hurry up, sweetheart!"

I threw my mobile on to the bed and raced downstairs.

Dad had done the cooking that evening. We were having sausage and mash, which was one of my favourites. We sat round the kitchen table and Mum and Dad bombarded me with questions about school, which was our usual evening routine.

As soon as I'd wolfed down my food, I made my excuses and escaped back upstairs, desperate to see if Nisha had texted.

I grabbed my phone off the bed and clicked into my messages. There was one from Nisha!

I haven't told her I saw it. I tried 2 talk 2 her but she won't come out of the bedroom...

It's OK. I'm sure the necklace will be there 2moro. x I replied.

I should've picked it up. She'll hate me when she finds out. :(

My heart sank. Things between Nisha and Poppy were complicated enough already! If the necklace was still in the changing room, it would be fine. But if it wasn't...? And if Poppy found out that Nisha had seen it and not picked it up, she'd probably never talk to her again. I needed to reassure Nisha that it would be OK, whether I believed it or not! I texted her back.

It'll be fine. Try not to worry. See u at school. x

True Colours

The next morning, Poppy and Nisha came into the classroom just as Miss Dubois arrived for registration, and so we didn't get a chance to talk. Nisha had texted Jas and Lexie, too, but they didn't know that Nisha hadn't told Poppy about spotting the necklace. I kept trying to catch Nisha's eye, but she had her head down and she wouldn't look at us.

Straight after registration, Poppy rushed off.

As we made our way to chemistry, I turned to Nisha. "What's happened? Did you go and look for the necklace this morning?"

"Yes. I pretended I was going to the toilet and I ran over to the changing rooms, but it's not there," Nisha said anxiously.

"Maybe someone handed it in…" Jas suggested.

Lexie and me nodded, but Nisha didn't seem convinced.

Poppy ran in to class five minutes late. "Sorry I'm late, I was—"

"Please just take your seat quietly, Poppy," Miss Dale said, looking over the rim of her glasses. "And turn to page forty-three in your textbook."

Poppy rushed to the bench, her books tipping out of her bag as she sat down. Miss Dale gave her a silencing look, then carried on teaching. Poppy's normal cool attitude seemed to have vanished. For the rest of the morning she stumbled through lessons, completely distracted. She disappeared at break and all through lunchtime, and she appeared at afternoon registration with swollen eyes, like she'd been crying.

Nisha took a deep breath, then turned to her as she sat down. "Are you all right, Poppy?"

Poppy's lip wobbled as she shook her head.

Miss Dubois walked into the classroom and clapped her hands. "*D'accord*, everyone, settle down, please," Miss Dubois began. "As you know, we have a policy here to not wear jewellery. But, it appears that Poppy was not aware of this rule. She has been wearing a necklace and it has been lost. She thinks it may have happened at some point yesterday, maybe during PE. It's a gold chain, with a heart-shaped locket, *oui*?" Poppy nodded miserably. "Could you all keep an eye out for it, please? If anyone finds it, please return it either to myself or to Poppy."

"Oh, I saw a necklace in the changing rooms yesterday," Kirsty piped up. "It was on the floor under the bench."

"Really?" Poppy asked, her face brightening.

"You saw it, too, didn't you, Nisha?" Kirsty continued, smirking. "In fact, you *knew* it was Poppy's, didn't you? But you didn't pick it up."

"You didn't?" Poppy breathed, turning to Nisha.

"Well, I..."

Poppy shook her head and ran out of the classroom, slamming the door behind her.

"Oh dear..." Kirsty said, swinging her leg innocently.

The loos are the place to be for a heart-to-heart...

The following day, Poppy was still looking miserable. She kept herself to herself and didn't even seem interested when Saskia and Nemone came over to talk about cheerleading.

"That necklace must have been seriously special if Poppy's so upset about it," Jas said, as we sat at our usual table in the dining hall.

"Have you got any idea why?" Lexie asked.

"None," Nisha said. "Poppy's gone completely silent at home with me, but I did overhear Dave talking to her about it last night at bedtime. He said he'd buy her a new one."

True Colours

"Oh well, that's sorted then," Jas said.

"Not quite," Nisha continued, "Poppy said it wouldn't be the same, that it could never be replaced... I feel terrible now."

Nisha fiddled with the strap on her bag.

"I know!" I piped up. "Why don't we try to find the necklace? It *must* be around somewhere."

"But Poppy's already looked," Nisha said miserably. "If *she* couldn't find it then I don't see how *we're* going to. Poppy hated me to begin with and now she's actually got a good reason to. I don't think she'll talk to me again – ever!"

"We could at least try and find it," Jas said, putting her arm round Nisha's shoulder and giving her a squeeze. "It's better than doing nothing!"

"Do you think we've even got a chance?" Nisha asked.

"Only one way to find out," Lexie said, grabbing Nisha's arm and heading off in the direction of the changing rooms.

So, whilst the rest of the school was flitting about in a whirl of giddy excitement about the Valentine's disco that evening, we were on our hands and knees in the changing rooms.

"Look!" Jas pointed under the bench. "There's a drain cover right next to where it was on the floor – maybe it slipped down there!"

Lexie wriggled under the bench on her front and I did the same. We took it in turns to pull at the drain cover, but it was stuck fast.

"Pull!" Lexie said, and we grabbed hold of it together, pulling with all our strength. Suddenly it made a sucking noise and popped out. We both shot up, banging our heads on the bench as the cover came free and giggling.

Jas grabbed the drain cover from the floor and waved it about in triumph. It was smelly, with clumps of slimy hair stuck to it.

"Eeewwww!" I squealed. "Get that away!"

Lexie peered down the hole.

"Can you see anything?" I asked.

"I need something to poke about with," she mumbled. "Can I borrow a pen or a pencil?"

Nisha grabbed an old pen from her pencil case and slid it under the bench to Lexie. Lexie prodded and poked about for a bit, while we all peered at the hole.

"I think I can see something shiny," she said quietly, concentrating for a second. "Bingo!"

True Colours

She shuffled back out, with a necklace covered in grime hanging off the end of Nisha's pen.

"That's it!" Nisha beamed, taking it carefully. "It's still got the heart-shaped locket on it. Look!"

The locket fell open.

"What's in it?" I asked, as we all crowded round, peering over Nisha's shoulder to look.

"A photograph," Nisha said, showing us. "It's Poppy with her mum and dad."

Poppy had long auburn hair in the photograph and she looked much younger. She was smiling really brightly.

"No wonder it means so much to her," Jas said. "She must really miss her mum and dad being together."

"I know how she feels," Nisha sighed.

We stood in silence for a second, looking at the picture. I took it for granted most of the time that Mum and Dad were together. I couldn't imagine them being apart, and having to only see one at a time.

"So, are you going to give it back to Poppy now?" Jas asked.

"I think it'd be better if I cleaned it first," Nisha said.

"You could give it back to Poppy at the disco tonight," I suggested.

"Good idea," Nisha replied, just as the bell rang. "And as you all helped me find it, can we give it back together?"

We nodded and, as we headed to registration, even I started to get excited about the disco!

By seven o'clock, the main hall had been transformed into a Valentine palace. Red paper hearts hung from the ceiling and coloured spotlights spun round the dancefloor. There was even a glitterball, casting twinkling light around the room. Me and Jas stood just inside the hall, looking for our friends.

The boys and girls from the older years looked totally cool and relaxed – unlike the Year Sevens and Eights. There were small groups of girls standing at the edges of the hall, looking over at the boys. A few of the boys had clearly made an effort and they looked totally awkward! Most of our year were already there, including Kirsty and Eliza. They looked sleek-haired and glamorous, and were pulling poses like they were back on the catwalk. They'd positioned themselves about halfway down the hall, near a group of Year Nine boys including Josh, Jas's brother. I looked round, but I couldn't see Nisha, Lexie or Poppy in the darkened hall.

Suddenly Jas's mobile beeped into life. "It's Nisha," she said as I leaned over to read it.

On way, just averted crisis!

We helped ourselves to a lemonade as we waited. Ed headed over, wearing his customary hoody, baggy jeans and trainers. He was grinning from ear to ear.

"All right?" he asked, as Jas nudged me and giggled. I nudged her back.

"Yup," I answered, glad the lights were down as I felt myself glow pink. "You?"

Ed nodded, and hung around for a bit like he was about to say something. Then he turned back into the crowds. But just before he disappeared, he called out, "Catch you later for a dance?"

He did a few moves, bumping into one of the Year Tens and spilling his drink down his hoody. Me and Jas shook our heads, as Zac's big laugh boomed out.

"Whatever you do, Jas, don't leave me on my own," I said, giggling. "We've got a deal to stick

together, remember?"

"Unless you change your mind and decide you *want* to dance with Ed, that is!" Jas replied, winking.

I smiled. "If I did, *you'd* probably have to dance with Zac!"

Finally Lexie and Nisha appeared. Nisha was wearing a cute sparkly dress. Lexie, on the other hand, looked pretty much the same as usual – she hadn't tried to recreate the look Poppy had given her at the disaster sleepover, but she looked really relaxed and happy.

"Poppy's just hanging up her coat," Lexie said.

"So, what was the crisis?" I asked.

"Oh, Poppy nearly refused to come," Nisha explained. "But Dave's out again and Mum's taken Callum over to one of his friend's houses for the evening. I'm nervous about giving her the necklace – I want to get it over with!"

"I just hope it cheers her up," Jas said. "I want tonight to be fun!" She was fidgeting as she spoke, moving her head to the music and clearly itching to dance.

Nisha and Lexie went to get drinks and we chatted to Zophia for a bit while we waited. By the time they got back, Poppy still hadn't turned up.

True Colours

"Do you think she's OK?" I said, checking my watch. "She's been ages."

"She's probably talking to Saskia and Nemone or something," Lexie said. But they were both dancing. Poppy wasn't anywhere in sight.

"We better check the cloakrooms," Jas suggested. We nipped out and headed down the spookily quiet corridors. We ducked into the cloakrooms, but they were empty.

"What about the toilets?" I asked. We went in and had a quick look round. We were about to go when I noticed that the furthest door was locked.

"Poppy?" I said, tapping gently on the door. The others came over. I heard a sniff from inside the cubicle. "Poppy, is that you?"

The lock scraped back and Poppy came out, her eyes red.

"What do you lot want?" she asked, seeing us all standing there. "Can't I just have a minute to myself?" She wiped her nose, giving Nisha a black look, then went to leave.

"We wanted to give you something," Nisha said quickly, reaching inside her dress pocket. "We found your necklace." She opened her hand and the gold

necklace lay there, sparkling.

Poppy gasped and reached out for it.

"The clasp's broken," Nisha explained. "That must be why it fell off when you got changed."

Poppy took the necklace carefully. "Thank you all so much!" She opened the locket, checking the picture.

"It's nice," Nisha said awkwardly. "The picture, I mean."

Poppy nodded, closing the locket up again. "It was the last birthday present I had from Mum and Dad before they..." She took a shaky breath. "Before they split up." Poppy ran the necklace through her fingers. "Two months later everything got turned upside down. We moved to London and I hardly saw Dad any more."

"So how come you weren't over the moon when you first got here?" Lexie asked. "You were getting to see your dad all the time."

"Oh, don't get me wrong, I was really happy to see *Dad*," Poppy said pointedly.

"But not me, though..." Nisha said.

Poppy looked up guiltily.

"It was pretty obvious," Nisha added, "but I still don't understand what I'd done."

Poppy looked unsure whether to say anything or

not. Then she let out a huge sigh. "You hadn't done anything wrong, I guess. It's just that Mum really struggles sometimes, when it's just the two of us. It feels like we're totally on our own. I mean, if something happens, like it did with Nan, there's no one else. That's because Dad's up here, in this brand-new family. You've got your mum *and* my dad. I hardly ever see him, while you get to live with him every single day. It doesn't feel fair." Poppy stared at her feet. "I was so ... so jealous of you for that. I hated it. I still do to be honest."

"But Dave's *your* dad, Poppy, not mine!" Nisha pointed out. "Your dad's great and everything, but I'd give anything to live with *my* dad every day, too. I hardly ever get to see him, either."

Poppy looked sheepish. "I didn't realize that till the concert last week," she admitted. "I ... I just thought you got to see your dad all the time, like you had the best of everything. I honestly felt terrible when you said you didn't see him. I'm so sorry I messed that up for you."

Nisha shrugged. "It's OK," she said with a small smile. "Well, not OK, but you know what I mean."

Poppy smiled back. "It's weird, though," she continued. "That first week with Dad was amazing.

But after that, he's been so busy with work that it felt more important than me."

"Tell me about it!" Nisha laughed. "I used to feel like that with my dad. But I've kind of got used to it now, and I understand how full on Dad's work is. Dave's the same, I guess."

"Sounds like you two have got more in common than you reckoned, Poppy," I pointed out.

"Exactly," Nisha smiled. "I know you thought I was a goody two-shoes, but I'm not perfect."

"I guess not," Poppy sighed. Then suddenly she frowned. "Hang on a sec, how did you know I thought you were a goody two-shoes?"

Nisha gulped and looked round desperately at me, Jas and Lexie. She spoke in a rush, looking worried. "Um, I'm really, really sorry – and don't hate me again – but I … I read your email to Angel by mistake. The one about me being boring and stuff. I didn't mean to, it's just you left it open..."

"No – I'm the one who should be sorry," said Poppy. "I was so mean about you in it because I wanted to hate you. I'm sorry for being so difficult and getting you into trouble. And I'm sorry for wrecking your fashion design, too, but it really was an accident, you know."

True Colours

"Well, I guess we *both* could have handled everything better." Nisha gave Poppy a small smile. "But let's just forget about it now."

The two step-sisters stood looking at each other uncertainly.

"Come on," Lexie piped up. "Can we go back to the hall now? We're missing everything!"

"Yes! And listen! They're playing 'Free'!" Jas cried. "We need to go and dance!"

"Nooooo!" Poppy groaned with a giggle. "Doesn't anyone have any decent music around here?"

We ran along the corridor and burst into the hall. The music and the heat enveloped us and we went straight to the dancefloor.

Poppy rolled her eyes at our moves. "You guys really need lessons," she joked. Then she started to dance. I noticed Luke glancing over. I had to give it to her, Poppy really could move.

Luke obviously thought the same thing. When the slow songs came on at the end of the disco, he walked over and asked Poppy to dance. Lexie nearly died with embarrassment and had to run to the loos to hide. Ed looked like he was heading over towards us, but Jas grabbed me and we rushed out of the hall to join Lexie,

giggling like mad!

When it got to half past nine, the time the disco was supposed to finish, Wiggy stopped the music and the teachers went around asking everyone to finish their drinks and start moving outside. We'd been having such a good time that we could hardly believe it was over already. Lots of the others must have felt the same, as no one was hurrying to go out and meet their parents!

Poppy and Luke were still standing on the dancefloor. They were talking to each other quietly and their noses were practically touching. We looked over and decided against going to interrupt them.

"Come on," Lexie said. "I definitely don't want to see them kiss! Let's go and get our coats and we can wait for them outside."

Kirsty and Eliza were in the cloakroom when we got there. They had their noses in the air and they looked seriously put out.

"Ugh, being asked to dance by Zac was the ultimate humiliation," Kirsty muttered as she pulled on her fluffy coat.

"For *him*," Eliza said, "when you said 'no way' really loudly!"

True Colours

I couldn't look the others in the eye without laughing, so we grabbed our coats and went straight out again.

Jas groaned. "Kirsty and Eliza need to learn how to have fun!"

"Yeah, I've had a great night hanging out with all of you," Nisha said. "And with Poppy!" she added with a little smile.

When Poppy finally came out of the hall, she was glowing. "That was the best disco ever!"

Nisha and Poppy –
step-sisters extraordinaire!

The next week flew by – it was the last week before the half-term holiday and we were counting down the days! Poppy helped Miss Malik and Nisha save Nisha's art project, making it almost as good as new. Poppy was really good fun once she finally let us get to know her. She still cringed at the stuff we didn't know, but only in a jokey way. She even taught us some of her dance moves. On Tuesday, Valentine's Day, she got one card. It had been slid into her locker and she found it before registration. Lexie said she felt sick as she recognized the writing – it was Luke's. Poppy grinned and told Lexie to get over it, in the nicest possible way!

Kirsty waltzed into the classroom, gloating. "Seven cards," she announced, smiling smugly. "And I'm sure I'll get loads more later, too."

Molly and Zophia had both got cards, and all of us tried to work out whose writing was in them. As we huddled round to look, I noticed that Travis was staring hard out of the window and Tom looked a bit shifty. He seemed to be taking more interest in his geography textbook than he had all year!

"How about you, Woody, did you get any?" Ed called over, looking a bit bashful.

I felt myself go crimson. Not only was Ed using my embarrassing nickname, but he was asking me about Valentine's cards! "As if I'd want any, anyway!" I mumbled back, trying to hide my face. But as I reached for my planner I spotted a bright pink envelope stuffed into my bag.

"Jas!" I squeaked in a panicked whisper. "Look! What do I do?"

"Er, open it?" Jas said. "I will, if you don't want to!"

She made a grab for the card, but I managed to wrestle it back – not before everyone had "oooohed" at me! Luckily Miss Dubois came in at that moment

and saved me… That meant I didn't have to open it in the classroom in front of everyone.

I sneaked a peek when we were on our way to the lab for chemistry, our first lesson. Inside there was a big question mark and the words "Will you be my Valentine?"

"It's so definitely from Ed!" Jas screamed. "He's your boyfriend!"

"No way!" I said, cringing. At that moment we saw Luke walk past, holding a card. He gave Poppy a small smile. She smiled back, while the rest of us tried to stifle our giggles!

The Luke and Poppy romance hotted up through the week. Not only was Poppy going to cheerlead at the football match that Luke was playing in on Saturday, but they even went out for a shake at the Ace Diner!

"I thought that wasn't cool enough for you," Lexie joked as Poppy got ready to go on Thursday after school.

"Depends who the company is," Poppy replied with a smile.

But then, just as Poppy was really starting to settle

in, everything was thrown up in the air again.

When we got into school on Friday morning, the last day before the half-term holidays, Poppy was in a complete tizz. First she dropped her coat, then her books and then she set off to registration in the completely wrong direction. Me and Jas thought it must be the effect that Luke was having on her, but Poppy and Nisha filled us in.

"Poppy's mum called last night," Nisha said.

"She's called every week," Poppy added, "to let me know how Nan's getting on. She's loads better, so I knew Mum would be coming home soon, I just didn't quite know when. Last night she announced that she's on her way home."

"What's the problem, then? I thought you'd be happy to escape this sleepy backwater as soon as you could!" Jas grinned.

"Oh, don't tell me, you've found true love with Luke and you can't bear to leave!" Lexie groaned dramatically.

Poppy wrinkled her nose. "Er, not quite," she joked. "But Mum wanted Dad to drop me off tomorrow."

"But it's the football match tomorrow!" I said. "You'd miss cheerleading!"

"Exactly my point!" Poppy laughed. "Luckily I managed to persuade Dad to take me home on Sunday instead. Mum was a bit disappointed, I think. Last time I spoke to her I couldn't wait to escape! Anyway, she's happy that I'm enjoying myself now."

"And we were wondering," Nisha added, "whether you three would come round for a sleepover, to say goodbye properly tomorrow night?"

"I promise there won't be any tantrums this time!" Poppy grinned. "Well, unless Mum changes her mind again that is!"

Nisha and Poppy finally looked happy hanging out together. I couldn't believe that after five weeks of torture, they were starting to get along, just as Poppy was about to disappear.

The football match was in the big park near to Lexie's house. The teams were already on the pitch when Jas and I arrived. We made our way through the crowd to Lexie and Nisha and huddled up together against the chilly February morning. As we waited for the game to start we waved to Poppy, who was standing over on the other side of the pitch between Saskia and

True Colours

Nemone and the other cheerleaders, all wearing their team uniform. They were jiggling about to keep warm.

The referee blew his whistle to start the match and the two teams began to play. Lexie did her best to explain the rules of the game to us, pointing out tackles and offside offences. Me, Jas and Nisha tried to pay attention, but before long we were chatting about our plans for the rest of the week and had stopped keeping track of the game. But even we heard the huge squeal that rang out, followed by a cheer. Luke had scored and Poppy almost leaped on to the pitch to celebrate!

As the half-time whistle blew, the teams left the pitch and the cheerleaders took their places. Poppy shook her pom-poms and twirled along with the others. She was totally confident with the routine – there was no way of telling that she'd only just joined. She even helped propel Nemone into the air to perform a somersault. They finished their display to massive cheers from the crowd. Poppy beamed at us and we clapped wildly. Jas snapped away on her camera, capturing every moment.

After the match, we hung around, waiting to say well done to Poppy. We eventually found her outside the changing-room block with Luke. They had their

phones out and it looked like they were swapping numbers. Then Luke actually leaned forward and kissed Poppy on the cheek. CRINGE!

When the two lovebirds had finally finished saying goodbye, we all split off. Nisha and Poppy went into town for a family lunch and Lexie, Jas and me snuck off to the shops to get a goodbye present for Poppy. Nisha had come up with the idea for what to get her and we were pretty sure that Poppy would love it – not like when we bought her welcome gifts!

Back at Nisha's that evening, we got out all our things for the sleepover in the living room. There were too many of us to fit in the bedroom, so Jamila and Dave had let us set up all the sleeping bags and pillows in there. We got into our PJs first and then snuggled down to watch a DVD. Jamila had made popcorn for us to snack on as we watched, and we did our best to keep it out of our sleeping bags!

As the end credits on the DVD came up, Nisha leaned behind the sofa and pulled out a pretty patterned bag. "We've got you a present," she said, handing it to Poppy. "Something to remember us by."

148

True Colours

"Oh, wow!" Poppy smiled, opening the bag and unwrapping the pink tissue paper. Inside was a photo frame with space for four photos. Jas had taken lots of pictures at the match earlier, and we'd got the best ones developed in town. There was one of all of us making faces at the camera, and one of Poppy and Nisha with Jamila, Dave and Callum. We'd put in one from the cheerleading display and the final picture was of Luke.

"This is amazing!" Poppy giggled. She looked up at us all. "It's really thoughtful – thank you."

"It was all Nisha's idea," Lexie said.

"Apart from the picture of Luke," Jas added. "I said that should be in there!"

We giggled.

"Do you know, I'm going to miss you all. I really didn't think I'd be saying that a week ago!" Poppy grinned at us.

"Maybe you could stay here, if you really like it that much?" I said.

Nisha and Poppy both opened their eyes wide, then laughed.

"Look, I like it here, don't get me wrong, but I don't think I'd go *that* far!" Poppy said.

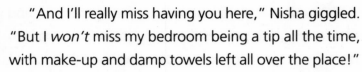

"And I'll really miss having you here," Nisha giggled. "But I *won't* miss my bedroom being a tip all the time, with make-up and damp towels left all over the place!"

"Yeah, sorry about that!" Poppy said. "Maybe I could visit, though? Not all the time, I mean," she added quickly, "but in holidays and stuff. That way I'd get to see more of Dad. And, more of you all, too."

"I'd really like that," Nisha smiled warmly.

For the first time since she'd arrived, Poppy leaned over and gave Nisha a huge hug.

"Don't be fooled, Nisha," Jas suddenly piped up. "Poppy might pretend that it's you she wants to visit, but we all know the truth!"

"What are you going on about?" Lexie asked.

"It's LUKE she wants to see!" Jas announced.

With that, Lexie shrieked and grabbed a pillow. "Pillow fight!"

Coming Soon!

Me and my BFFs have made a pact to follow our dreams. Jas is set to be a **STAR**, Nisha works **MAGIC** with a camera and my **DREAM** is to be a reporter… That just leaves Lexie – she wants to be a footballer, but not everyone is taking her ambition seriously.

There's **NO WAY** she's going to be left on the touchline…

Lexie is on a mission!

Have you read?

Holly Robbins

BFFs

Sink or Swim

Me and my BFF, Jas, are moving up to secondary school and I've got a zillion **MAJOR FEARS**… Like looking a total dork in my **MASSIVE** uniform … being teased about my **EMBARRASSING** surname … and getting completely **LOST** on my way to lessons! And I'm sure I'll be one of the youngest (and shortest) in the **WHOLE** school.

But my biggest, most **HUMONGOUS** fear of all is that Jas will realize that I'm not cool and find herself a new BFF.

I think I need a popularity makeover – and fast!

Have you read?

Me and my BFFs, Jas, Lexie and Nisha, are all **SUPER EXCITED** about our school play, especially Jas. She's always dreamed of being on the stage and she has her sights set on a **STAR PART**! Trouble is, she's now so **TOTALLY OBSESSED** that it's turned her into a bit of a **DIVA**.

If she's not careful our **FRIENDSHIP PACT** will be ruined…

Jas needs a major reality check!